The
Connoisseur

Evan S. Connell, Jr.

AVON
PUBLISHERS OF BARD, CAMELOT AND DISCUS BOOKS

Grateful acknowledgment is made to the following for permission to reprint previously published material:

Holle-Verlag: For two brief excerpts from *Pre-Columbian Art & Later Indian Tribal Arts* by Ferdinand Anton and Frederick J. Dockstader (1968 Harry N. Abrams, Inc.).

The Metropolitan Museum of Art: For an excerpt from *Before Cortés: Sculpture of Middle America*, copyright © 1970 by The Metropolitan Museum of Art.

Simon & Schuster, Inc.: For excerpts from *Art Before Columbus* by André Emmerich and Lee Boltin (1963 Simon & Schuster, Inc.).

AVON BOOKS
A division of
The Hearst Corporation
959 Eighth Avenue
New York, New York 10019

First Avon Printing, June, 1977

To Robert Gottlieb

Id quod visum placet.

Thomas Aquinas

UNSPEAKABLE dignity isolates the diminutive nobleman. Dominating the shelf, his regnant nature ignores the bric-a-brac obstructing his view. With arms folded and head imperially lifted he waits cross-legged for the next petitioner. God help that supplicant.

Muhlbach, astonished, has paused. I want this arrogant little personage, he thinks with sudden passion. But why? Does he remind me of myself. Or is there something universal in his attitude? Well, it doesn't matter. He's coming home with me.

The mistress of the shop approaches. She, too, has folded her arms—either in unconscious emulation or, more likely, against the cold New Mexico morning.

I see you've taken a fancy to our magistrate.

Muhlbach replies with a noncommittal murmur.

Together they contemplate the remote lord. His features, although indistinct, look Negroid. His cheeks have been ritually scarified and he sports a goatee. He wears a simple robe without a belt, a necklace of clay pellets, circular earplugs, and an elaborate coiling headdress terminating in half a dozen spikes—two of which are broken.

Give him a tap with your fingernail.

Muhlbach does so. The tiny statue rings like porcelain.

Tell me, what is this?

She misinterprets the question. Terra cotta—though nearly everyone takes it for bronze.

But where is it from?

Mexico. I thought you knew.

And where is the original?

I beg your pardon?

This must be a replica. Isn't the original in some museum?

Oh, no no! No, indeed. This is not a reproduction. This is authentic. If it were a copy I would tell you. The piece is from the Mayan period and is quite old. I should guess at least five hundred years.

Well, he thinks, bending down for a closer look, I'm afraid I won't be buying it after all. It must cost a young fortune. You say this is a 'magistrate'?

We just call him that. Good Heavens, nobody knows who or what he actually represents. Of course the anthropologists are constantly digging away at these pre-Columbian cultures so eventually we may get some sort of idea. Summer before last my sister and I vacationed in Yucatán and our guide proved to be of Mayan descent, which made us feel almost as though we were in touch with the past. And visiting the ruins of Chichén Itzá—now that was a thrill! We'd like nothing better than to go back, but there's the expense.

Yes, there's always that.

By the way, I am Mrs. Soquel.

Muhlbach introduces himself.

Are you from the East, Mr. Muhlbach?

New York.

What brings you to Taos?

Business.

Mrs. Soquel moves a step closer. What line of business, may I ask?

Insurance. Metropolitan Mutual Life and Casualty.

She pretends to find this quite unusual. Would you be opening an office in Taos?

No. We have been studying the feasibility of a merger with Occidental Life which has branch offices in a number of your western states. At any event, since I happened to be in Albuquerque and had heard that Taos was a picturesque artists' colony I decided to rent a car and drive up.

I'm glad you did. What impressions have you formed?

It certainly is quiet.

I suppose it must seem that way to a New Yorker, though to us it seems to be growing dreadfully noisy. What do you think of the landscape?

Extraordinary.

Tourists usually say 'spectacular.' October is the nicest month, at least in my opinion. The aspens are gorgeous. You must try to visit us in the fall.

I'm sure it's beautiful. Has Taos always been your home?

Oh, no. I was born in Grand Junction, Colorado, but my parents moved to Santa Fe when I was a child. That was where I later had the good fortune to meet Mr. Soquel. We lived thirty years in Santa Fe—years I shall never forget. He was the eldest son of Judge Soquel, of whom you may have heard.

Muhlbach, who has not heard of the eminent judge, nods politely.

Mrs. Soquel goes right along, one sunbrowned hand pressed to her cheek, chatting as though they have known each other for a long time. After the death of her husband she felt a need to escape so she moved to Taos and persuaded her sister, who lived in Fort Collins and whose husband simply was no good, to join her. She has never regretted the move, although her sister often speaks of returning to Fort Collins.

Muhlbach picks up the statue because Mrs. Soquel, once started, is difficult to stop. And as he studies the imperturbable figure he again feels the urge to buy it.

She holds out a magnifying glass which must be one of the largest in the world. The handle is half the size of a baseball bat and the diameter of the lens implies that anything from microbes to the northern hemisphere might be scrutinized.

Under the lens the Mayan's features grow more distinct and, if possible, more uncompromising. Even the striations of his goatee are visible. Where the spikes have been snapped off the fine red granular texture of the clay can be seen.

Mrs. Soquel, drifting closer, makes a suggestion. Look between the third and fourth spikes.

He does. There he perceives a deposit of incredibly vivid blue paint.

Much of it must have been like that. Now look on the left side of the robe. You'll observe a grayish residue. We suspect that area was originally the same color, or perhaps white with a blue design. The famous Maya blue.

You seem to be an authority on these things.

She waves one hand in a deprecatory gesture. I do know our local pottery, of course, having lived here forever and ever. But as for being an authority on pre-Columbian—oh, I'm afraid not.

Muhlbach inspects the base of the statue, which is flat except for two coils of clay representing the legs. Traces of a yellow gummy substance adhere to the coils.

That would be adhesive, she explains. Beeswax, I should guess, which somebody put there so it wouldn't topple over. We used to get quite a number of these—oh, I can recall when we would have five or six. Not anymore. They're scarce as hen's teeth.

Well, he thinks, that means I can't afford it. He puts the figure back on the shelf.

Mrs. Soquel continues with hardly a pause.

Some years ago we had the loveliest Mayan lady in a white cloak. She was carrying a little dog and leading a child by the hand. I don't know how long she was in the shop until my sister said all right, since nobody wants to buy her let's just take her home. Today we'd have no trouble disposing of that item because so many people are collecting antiques. But you never can tell what's going to become popular. Margaret suspects contemporary Indian pottery may go up next. San Ildefonso and Santa Clara especially. But in any case, my grandson knocked over that lovely white figure and we never did get around to repairing it. We kept pieces in a shoebox and every now and then reminded ourselves, but you know how it is with good intentions. I haven't laid eyes on that box for months. Margaret may have put it out with the trash. She was always the neat one. People like to say I'm tidy but I never could hold a candle to Margaret. She ran up to Questa for the morning.

I see. Well, what about this fellow? How much are you asking?

Thirty dollars.

Did you say thirty?

Yes. Actually that's not unreasonable.

I know nothing whatever about these things. Nothing. But I must admit that does sound reasonable.

A guarantee goes with it, of course.

A guarantee?

Of authenticity. So many pre-Columbian figures are being faked. I'm sure you must be aware of that.

No. No, I'm not.

Runners come through all the time. You've got to be careful.

Runners?

Smugglers. We call them runners. Sometimes they have authentic pieces but most often it's junk.

She takes a moment to rearrange the shawl about her shoulders. A dense pleasant odor like overly ripe peaches seems to fill the cool silence. Muhlbach, slightly hypnotized, realizes that he has been staring at her. In a matronly way she's not unattractive. In fact she's quite handsome. Her glossy black hair streaked with gray is parted in the center, drawn back to emphasize her profile. Her skin looks brown and healthy, a bit crinkled from years in the New Mexico sun. Her deep pendulous bosom and both arms are loaded with heavy silver and turquoise. Indian jewelry. Her voice is vibrant, almost theatrical.

You must excuse me, she remarks after touching her nose with a handkerchief. I'm recuperating from the flu.

Really? I'm surprised. I shouldn't think anyone would get sick in this part of the country.

We often hear that. I can't imagine why. People from the cities drive through and talk as though it were Paradise. No offense, Mr. Muhlbach.

Then she smiles, showing the tip of a large pink tongue.

He blinks and clears his throat. No, of course not. Now about this business of fakes. You say you are able to distinguish the authentic items?

It can be difficult. Margaret's eye is better than my own, even so we almost never buy from runners. We don't deal primarily in pre-Columbian, as you see. And if we do have a piece it's usually through a friend who can vouch for the authenticity.

He looks around the shop. Cactus candy, scented candles, tie clasps in the shape of a horse's head, giant postcards, manufactured moccasins, pomegranate jelly, desert incense—whatever that may be—scenic place mats, petrified wood bookends, varnished copper ashtrays and all the rest of it. A hundred miles from Route 66, he thinks, but there's still a market for rubbish. One would suppose that the presence of mountains and forests and these indescribable plateaus might elevate the public taste, but evidently not.

When he looks at the Mayan figure again the contrast is startling.

Why hasn't anybody bought this? I should think it would have sold very quickly.

I was about to tell you. This piece was sold several months ago, but just the day before yesterday it was returned. Whenever we handle pre-Columbian we make sure the purchaser understands that he may return it if the authenticity is questioned. Margaret and I both feel that we gain more than we lose by this policy.

Now let me get it straight, says Muhlbach. Somebody bought that figure but returned it to you because he suspected it was not genuine?

That is correct. A gentleman from Alamogordo purchased it in July, I believe. Or late June—I'd have to look. Then just recently, if we are to believe his tale, some friend chanced to see it and insisted that it was a copy.

So you refunded his thirty dollars?

Oh, yes. At once.

Do you still guarantee the object?

Absolutely. I've already told you.

Well, says Muhlbach after a pause, I have another question. The friend of this gentleman from Alamogordo—how did he determine that it was a copy?

Mrs. Soquel doesn't know. She didn't inquire. People are so timid, she continues. You can frighten most of them out of their wits without half trying.

That friend of his told him it wasn't possible to buy an authentic Jaina for thirty dollars so he must have thought we'd taken advantage of him. I didn't ask any questions because I have no patience with such people. I'd just be wasting my breath. Margaret feels the same. We are thoroughly honest and we have no desire to argue.

Jaina?

Jaina, she explains, is the name of a small island off the coast of Campeche which was used as a burial ground by the Mayans. These terra cotta figurines have been discovered only on that island, not at any other site. According to Mr. Coe it may have been a royal necropolis.

Who is Mr. Coe?

Mr. Coe is an authority on Mayan culture.

I see. Well, I want to buy this. Regardless of whether or not it's authentic, I like it very much. You needn't bother about the guarantee.

I knew you were planning to take it. I could tell right away.

I had no idea my intentions were so obvious.

Yes, indeed. Margaret and I learned long ago to read the customer's mind.

Muhlbach opens his wallet and counts thirty dollars into her brown southwestern palm.

Now the governor will want his pennies, she remarks in that husky flu-affected voice, so let me just add it up.

She goes on talking as she walks around the counter with an unhurried queenly swaying motion rather like a yacht sailing through a tranquil sea:

If you've any doubts about the piece you could have it authenticated at the university in Albuquerque. The anthropology department is considered quite good. You'll be passing the university on your way to the airport.

Muhlbach, half convinced that they both are actors in a Taos Little Theater production, hears himself reply:

That won't be necessary.

Good for you! Mrs. Soquel exclaims, looking up with dramatic suddenness. I like people who think for themselves. I'm so tired of namby pambies. Now let me rummage around for some tissue and a box to put this in.

She disappears through a beaded curtain.

He wanders toward the front window where he stops with a meditative expression, hands clasped behind his back. On the opposite side of the street a huge icicle sparkles in the morning sun and it occurs to him that he might live in Taos. What would it be like? What would a person do day after day? There seems to be no industry. No entertainment except the movie on the plaza. Night-clubs? Not likely. Roadhouses along the highway serving beer and country music. Seventy miles to Santa Fe which might be a little more active, though not much.

He peers up the street. Three Indians wrapped in pale green and pink Montgomery Ward blankets stand like mummies on the sagging snowy boardwalk. What a curious town.

Mrs. Soquel, heralded by the sound of clattering beads, sails grandly through the curtain. She has some string, a handful of excelsior and a cigar box.

He's not as fragile as you might think. However we won't take chances.

You've been here a long time, Mrs. Soquel. You must be satisfied with life in Taos.

I couldn't abide any other place. Margaret drove to Albuquerque last spring and says it's become impossible. No, thank you, I'll stay put. You can keep your big cities.

You feel no sense of isolation?

From what, Mr. Muhlbach? Come here and put your finger on this knot.

Obediently he walks to the counter.

There! she exclaims. That's a darling. Now, would you like it in a bag?

No, this should do fine. Just out of curiosity, what would my magistrate cost in New York?

Goodness, I've never been to New York. Quite something, though. A hundred dollars, maybe more. They say pre-Columbian prices have skyrocketed.

Then why are you willing to sell it for so little? Or let me ask the question another way. Wouldn't it pay you to ship the piece to a gallery in New York?

I suppose, but we were able to buy it for next to nothing so we can sell it for almost nothing.

She walks to the door beside him, settling the bright shawl, and a bracelet gleams against her sturdy female wrist. The odor of her body is intoxicating. Muhlbach is almost overcome. At this moment anything seems possible.

By the door she hesitates. Then she holds out her hand.

Goodby. Next time you visit Taos do stop in.

Yes, he answers, eager to grasp both of those plump capable hands. Yes, he will look forward to it.

Outside the shop he squints at the cerulean sky while pulling on his gloves. The air is warmer. The icicles have begun to melt. The Indians haven't moved, except that they are watching him. It occurs to Muhlbach that his black New York overcoat and homburg and thin-soled city shoes must look absurd. He considers nodding to the Indians but it would be like trying to communicate with a previous century.

Carrying the cigar box in one hand he strides up

the boardwalk. Past an art gallery featuring lavender mountains, past the Taos bookshop, the Kit Carson house, another art gallery. And then a lean old rancher with a broken nose and a jaw like a trowel comes clumping along, suitably armored for a New Mexico January—boots caked with mud, denims, a thick sheepskin jacket, the inevitable Stetson. The brim of his Stetson has been rolled at the sides. In Denver the hats were rolled to a point in front creating a triangular effect. So it seems there are fashions even in the primeval West.

Good morning.

Howdy.

Howdy! Muhlbach thinks, walking unevenly across the frozen ruts, feeling the eyes of the three Indians like feathered arrows in the back of his neck. Great Lord, what next?

On the way to Albuquerque he studies the trees beside the road, wondering which might be aspens. October, she said. October. Could I come back next October? Why not? I want to. Or maybe I'm losing my mind. I just spent thirty dollars for something I would never have noticed in New York.

He glances at the cigar box on the seat. Is the Mayan really five centuries old? Probably not. It must be a clever fraud. He pats it affectionately.

Twenty minutes later the canyon opens up and he emerges on the plateau. The scope of the West is alarming. The eternal emptiness. Silence. Perhaps so much snow accounts for that eerie silence. Whatever the reason, New Mexico seems to disclaim humanity. The existence of a man, or of an army of men, is irrelevant. A quiet snowy field in Pennsylvania, for example, wouldn't be at all like this.

Through Española, much less attractive than its name, and Pojoaque, not listed on the map as one of the Principal Towns, and a sandstone moonscape populated with trailer homes. Then up the long bleak grade through an undernourished ever-green jungle—the limbs and trunks of the desperate trees strangely black against the snow. Then the futuristic opera house, over the crest and down toward Santa Fe.

Well, he remarks aloud, I just don't know about this.

But his own voice, familiar and moderate though it may be on the streets of New York, sounds harsh.

Dead ahead the Sandia Mountains have begun to rise from the plateau like a stage set. He decides not to say anything else. Half an hour, he thinks. Forty minutes at most. The plane doesn't leave till six, which means several hours with nothing to do. I should have stopped in Santa Fe. I could have had lunch and wandered around. Well, what about lunch?

He consults the road map.

Bernalillo is the only town in heavy type. But it's not much farther to Albuquerque. All right, keep going. Driving is easier than stopping. The scenery is hypnotic. Yes, the scenery. Canyons. Mountains. Forests. That must be what holds these people, makes them the way they are.

All at once he realizes that four or five cars have shot past dangerously unnoticed. He shakes his head and sits erect.

The Sandia peaks are no longer a cardboard cut-out. The first Albuquerque billboards are approaching.

He looks at his watch. After lunch, what?

A billboard invites him to ride the aerial tram-way. The next suggests a stay at the newly reno-vated Vaquero motel with color TV in every room. Cocktail lounge. 24 hour coffee shop. Heated swim-ming pool. Minutes from downtown. Commercial rates. Children welcome.

The first freeway sign appears, miles ahead of

any construction. The city fathers must be anticipating a megalopolis on this stupefying plateau.

By the time he has reached the Central exit he knows what to do with part of the afternoon.

At the stop light he turns confidently downhill toward the university. Several blocks later, approaching the railroad overpass, he admits that it must be the opposite direction. All right, around the block and up Central past the exotic promise of a thousand and one motels.

And suddenly there it is, the deep brown adobe buildings just visible through a slender growth of pines. He locates a parking spot near the anthropology department and stiffly unfolds himself from the rented Volkswagen.

Classes are letting out. The campus is bright with mackinaws and checkered wool shirts. Red. White. Purple. Yellow. To be here with an armload of books, to be entering life through this colorful gate—Muhlbach, middle-aged, conservative and dignified in his black overcoat, glasses riding the bridge of his narrow patrician nose, stops for a moment on the frozen path to contemplate the long-haired bearded boys and the girls in jeans. How extraordinarily young they are.

Four boys approach. Why do they look different from boys in the East? It must be those wool shirts. And the boots. But something else. Ah! The belts. Western belts with huge silver buckles.

A professor comes down the path. Unmistakably a professor. Gray hair neatly trimmed, no beard. And somehow he seems to walk against the years instead of with them. One step, then the next. He carries a scarred leather satchel with a broken hasp, a veteran satchel, handy for textbooks, term papers, et cetera. So much for three decades in the service of Higher Education. Or so little, depending on one's viewpoint.

The professor walks by without looking up.

Take care, Muhlbach silently advises him. Watch your step, because there's ice on the path.

Inside the anthropology building he has no idea where to go. The corridor is lined with display cabinets: Paleolithic arrowheads, Pleistocene skulls, flints, spears, pots, baskets, diagrams, photographs of pygmies and—most unexpected—three elaborately decorated ostrich eggs. He bends down for a closer look at the eggs.

Just then a woman carrying a sheaf of papers walks out of an auditorium. She appears to be a secretary. He decides to follow her.

She enters an office. Fine. This must be the place.

After taking off his hat and gloves he taps on the door, then steps inside to explain. He bought a small clay figure this morning in Taos. The lady who sold it—a Mrs. Soquel—suggested that somebody here might be able to examine it.

Unfortunately, the head of the department isn't in today and Dr. Romero has a class.

I realize this is presumptuous, but I'm leaving very soon for New York. Wouldn't there be anybody?

The secretary is doubtful.

Chuck Quimby is here. Let me see.

She picks up the phone and Muhlbach is surprised to find himself listening anxiously.

The conversation is brief. Just that one piece? Yes. Okay.

You're in luck, Mr. Muhlbach. If you will go down the corridor and turn right Mr. Quimby will be waiting for you.

Quimby, who must be seven feet tall, looks like a stork about to take flight. Dressed in a lab technician's smock that flaps around his knees, holding a pair of tweezers as though he was ready to pluck out somebody's eye, he beckons from the entrance to his office. His expression is altogether humorless.

Muhlbach walks into the office with an uneasy feeling, prepared to explain about Taos and what Mrs. Soquel had said. Quimby is not interested.

What have you got? he demands in a resonant bass voice without moving his lips.

Muhlbach tries to open the box, but Mrs. Soquel must have been a sailor because nobody will ever untie that knot. He begins to feel ridiculous. He glances at Quimby, who slowly reaches out with a penknife and cuts the string.

The Mayan lies on his back staring at the ceiling with utter contempt, his goatee protruding through a few strands of excelsior.

Quimby doesn't say a word.

I've been stung, Muhlbach thinks. I bought a fake.

Quimby plucks the statue from its nest and sets it upright. After a few seconds he bends down from his tremendous height like a giant in a fairy tale and taps the tiny figure several times with an automatic pencil.

Muhlbach frowns. This tapping business must indicate something, but what?

Quimby stares at the Mayan. Suddenly a jeweler's glass no bigger than a thimble materializes in his enormous hand.

Muhlbach looks at it with astonishment. Where did it come from? What became of the pencil? And the penknife—where did the knife go? And the tweezers? Where are the tweezers? Ah ha! Those pockets in the smock. Yes, of course.

Quimby and the Mayan are face to face like determined antagonists with the jeweler's glass wedged between them.

Muhlbach watches respectfully.

Around the arrogant Mayan's head, down the folded arms and up again, over the earplugs and the necklace and the coiled spikes, back and forth, pausing here and there, up and down the length of the robe.

At last a rumbling noise can be heard.

However, it seems that the anthropologist was just clearing his throat; he is not yet ready to announce a verdict. He turns the Mayan around in order to examine the back. Next he investigates the base.

The telephone rings, but he pays no attention. Muhlbach feels encouraged.

After the phone has rung half a dozen times Quimby answers: Yes? Mmm, no.

He hangs up.

Muhlbach decides that the secretary has called to find out if the piece is authentic. But that's not likely. The call must have been about something else.

I suppose you noticed—there appears to be some kind of yellow gum on the bottom, probably beeswax. I wondered if that might be significant.

Mmm, says Quimby, who is now holding a dental pick.

Muhlbach glances at his pocket because the pick must have come from there, unless he had it up his sleeve.

Quimby works gently at the base of the statue. Then he peers through the jeweler's glass. His lips twitch. He sets the Mayan down beside the cigar box.

Moments go by as slowly as minutes. Muhlbach begins to feel that he himself, and not the little statue, is on trial.

Quimby rumbles again. Is he ready to speak? Yes.

I would have no doubts about this. This is authentic.

Really? Well, that's good news. That's very good news indeed. But why did you tap it with a pencil?

Bad ones sound like lead.

I suspected something of the sort. And what did you find out by scratching it?

Quimby answers that the Mayans used a finely ground clay. They were good craftsmen. Fakers are not often so meticulous.

Well! thinks Muhlbach. All I need is a jeweler's glass and a dental pick.

It would be from the island of Jaina, is that correct?

Who said it was from Jaina?

The lady in Taos who sold it to me. She knows quite a lot about these things.

Mmm, says Quimby.

In your opinion where would it be from?

It could be Jaina. Leave your address. I'll send you a note.

Muhlbach hands him an engraved card which he drops into a pocket.

Do you need more time to examine it?

Quimby shakes his head.

Could you estimate its age?

I'll let you know.

He's acting peevish, Muhlbach thinks. All right. I appreciate the information, Mr. Quimby.

He puts the Mayan in the cigar box, tucks some excelsior over it and shuts the lid.

Quimby holds out a thick red rubber band.

What else does he carry in those pockets? Muhlbach wonders while stretching the rubber band around the box. A collapsible silk hat? Colored scarves? White rabbits?

You know, Mr. Quimby, when I was a boy I wanted to become an archaeologist. As a matter of fact, when my grandfather was on his deathbed he presented me with an archaeology book. I've always been fascinated by the subject. Somehow I just never had the leisure to pursue it.

Quimby listens attentively, but doesn't answer.

He's cold, Muhlbach tells himself. As cold as any bird I've met. Nevertheless I like him. And he knows what he's doing. Too bad he's not more communicative, I'd like to stay and talk a while. But at least I found out what I came here to find out.

Once again, thank you. I hope I haven't taken too much of your time.

The anthropologist murmurs some undecipherable pleasantry through those bloodless lips. Already he appears to be thinking about other matters. A draft from the open door lifts the tail of his smock, causing it to wave benevolently as though saying goodby.

Muhlbach starts out.

Mmm, Quimby remarks. Bushnell or Dockstader might be in your library.

And then for a few minutes the taciturn giant becomes talkative. Ekholm. Hasso von Winning. Kidder. Lothrop. Coe. Proskouriakoff. From his magic pocket he takes a scratchpad in order to jot down the names.

Good. I'll want something to read on the plane. How about your campus bookstore?

Quimby tells him where to find it.

On route to the bookstore he realizes that he has not had lunch. Well, there should be time enough for a drive out to the old plaza which supposedly has some decent restaurants. Certainly there wasn't much along Central—pizza parlors, fish-and-chips, soda fountains, Okie's Rathskeller across from the university, probably a student hangout, and something called the Munch Inn. Then there was the Presbyterian Hospital in case one could use a stomach pump. All right, pick up a book and then a visit to 'Old Town' as they call it.

On display at the bookstore is a handsome volume of pre-Columbian art from the National Museum of Anthropology in Mexico City. It has quite a few pictures and should be easy reading. Just what the doctor ordered. Also displayed is a book by one of the authorities Quimby mentioned—Dockstader. Dr. Frederick J. Dockstader in collaboration with a Dr. Anton. Muhlbach riffles the pages and turns to the index. Huaca, Huarez, Ica, Isthmus, Jaguar, Jaina . . .

So there actually is such a place. Not only that, Dockstader and Anton devote five pages to it. Mildly surprised, he begins to read:

Off the coast of the Yucatán peninsula, on the arid island of Jaina in the Gulf of Campeche, are two ruined Maya pyramids. In the Maya language of Yucatán, Jaina means 'The-House-over-the-Sea.' But the tiny island does not owe its fame to these pyramids, but rather to the lovely grave offerings which have been dug up by the hundreds and which afford us a glimpse of a long vanished but splendid past.

That's sufficient. He takes both books.

At the cash register he asks for directions to Old Town.

You can't miss it, according to the clerk. Straight out Central.

Downtown Albuquerque may not be any more exotic than downtown Hackensack, although it's less congested. In fact, Albuquerque's business district gives the impression of being in a recession and Muhlbach drives along the main street with a bemused smile. Not a taxicab in sight. No subway. Plenty of parking space. One turquoise-colored municipal bus marked 'Winrock,' almost empty. Five or six indolent citizens wait for a traffic light to change. The First National Bank seems to be the skyscraper—perhaps eight floors. Maisel's, apparently an Indian souvenir shop. Woolworth's. Dan's Boots and Saddles. More dimestores. Kress. McLellan's.

By Tenth Street this stunning commercial avenue

has been replaced by the ubiquitous laundromat, the cut-rate motel, the Dairy Queen and Tastee Freez, the terrible suggestiveness of an Eddieburger. And by quite a few vacant lots.

A snow-covered lot for sale instead of a fluorescent honeycomb staffed with secretaries and executives. So much unoccupied space. This may be what I'll remember, he tells himself. Yes, and the silence. My God, where are the crowds and the fights? Why doesn't anything happen? If I lived here would I go mad or become infatuated with the place?

Lunch on the Old Town plaza consists of eggs scrambled with chiles, half a pound of refried beans, and buns filled with air—called *sopaipillas*—which one covers with syrup. For dessert there's a cup of baked caramel custard, scorched but tasty, called *flan*. All this and a civil waitress for two dollars. There are, he reflects while paying the bill, several reasons I might pack up and move West. I won't, of course. I can't. It's impossible. But I can enjoy the thought.

After lunch he wanders across the plaza marveling at the spectacle of snow unmixed with soot, stops to inspect two old cannons near the bandstand, and notices the trail of his own footprints. It occurs to him that until the snow melts, or new snow falls, his tracks will remain in this plaza. And although he cannot imagine why, the idea is rather gratifying.

Late that afternoon, somewhat fatigued, carrying his books on pre-Columbian art, his suitcase and a cigar box secured with a red rubber band, he passes solemnly through the Albuquerque Sunport.

Vast shadows have begun to reach across the mesa when the plane takes off.

With his forehead pressed against the small cold oval window he looks down. Only one highway curves around the desolate Sandia peaks. He follows it, trying to locate Santa Fe. And farther north at the base of a blunt mountain a strand of lights could be Taos.

Presently the mountains give way to midwestern plains. He opens Dr. Dockstader's book.

But before starting to read he considers the events that have led one right after another like footprints to such an unexpected conclusion. A prosaic business trip, a bit of extra time, the recollection of a tourist brochure about Taos—and here I am, he thinks, flying home with a pre-Columbian clay idol. Now nothing just 'happens' in this world, yet for the life of me I cannot imagine why I walked into Mrs. Soquel's shop. I got to Quimby because of what she said, that's true, and because of Quimby I bought these books, so I suppose it's logical. Nevertheless, it's peculiar.

His thoughts return to Quimby, whose examination of the statue may have been somewhat superficial. How could he be sure the piece was genuine? He didn't study it very long, less than ten minutes. All he did was listen to the noise it made and look at the surface. He didn't equivocate. He said 'I would have no doubts about this. This is authentic.' So the question must be whether or not he knows his stuff.

Yet why do I care about authenticity? What difference does it make? When I bought the figure I assured Mrs. Soquel that I wanted it because I liked it, not because she was willing to guarantee it. If that was enough for me this morning, why shouldn't it be enough this evening?

Just then the stewardess inquires if he would care to purchase a cocktail.

Yes. A martini with two olives.

After making a note of his order she tips her head to indicate that she is reading the title of his book.

My! That sounds fascinating!

She moves along the aisle and he listens to her next conversation:

Would you care to purchase a cocktail?

Double Scotch on the rocks.

Yes, sir. Oh! I see you're a crossword puzzle fan!

Muhlbach looks out the window. A full moon is rising, the night is clear. The midwestern plains seem less monotonous by moonlight. In fact, the landscape is quite lovely—a dark silvery monochrome reminiscent of a scene by one of those early American painters. Blakelock or Ryder, perhaps. Frozen lakes gleam for a moment as brilliantly as metal mirrors, then vanish with a flash beneath the wing. How would it feel to be an artist, to spend one's life observing the earth and the things that grow on it and attempting to communicate those observations? Take that little clay personage—how skillfully executed, how sensitive. How profoundly endowed with a knowledge of humanity its creator must have been.

The stewardess returns with his drink. After a few sips he switches on the overhead lamp, locates the passage he had begun in the campus bookstore, and continues reading:

The Jaina terra cottas can be called the Meissen ware of the New World. The figures, mostly of priests, princes, and warriors, are of a harmonious beauty, classic in form and conception. Their calm expression and dignified bearing suggest an aristocratic self-possession. The modeling of the bodies is restricted to essentials, although it is strongly dynamic, whereas the garments and ornaments which characterize the subject's social rank are worked out in the finest detail. Probably the impressionistic treatment of the bodies was deliberate: it may be that the artists wished to infuse the figures with a breath of that life which death had taken from them—Jaina was not a home for the living, it was an isle of the dead. Most of the dead there were buried in a crouching position, and in their mouths were often placed a bead of jade, the stone the Mayans valued higher than gold. In their hands were placed these tiny statuettes which today are sought after as precious rarities.

On the same page is a color photograph of a prince seated on his jaguar throne. Height 4″, late classic period, according to the footnote. The prince wears a sophisticated conical hat and a fancy dress cloak with patches of blue paint.

More than a thousand years, Muhlbach thinks. Astonishing. This was made at about the time Charlemagne ruled France.

He studies the prince critically, comparing it with his own little masterpiece. They are almost the same size. The one in the book has more paint and its features seem not quite so blurred by centuries of burial. It's better, no sense denying the fact. Yes, the one in the book is better. But still, mine is good.

On the adjoining page is a couple. Height 7″. Unusually large. And probably very valuable. Quite a lot of that blue paint, especially on the woman's skirt. Both figures are in good condition, missing a few fingers and toes, the spikes of their hats are broken, and the right side of the woman's face has been eroded. But there doesn't seem to be any serious breakage. Nevertheless, the hands look clumsy— not altogether pleasing. I must say I prefer my nobleman.

He turns the page and finds a fat warrior carrying a small round shield. Naked from the waist up. Earplugs. A huge necklace with what appear to be a couple of human bones as the pectoral attraction. The warrior's lips are parted and his head is tilted as though listening. He looks very much like a North American Indian.

Then on the next page Muhlbach sees a Mayan dignitary so similar to the one in the cigar box that for a few moments all he can do is stare at it. The pose is identical—that arrogant lift to the head, the folded arms, legs crossed beneath a broad sash. The headdress is almost the same. Both have scarified cheeks, although the pattern is different. They wear the same garment—a robe or skirt of some sort. The one in the book wears a simple rope necklace terminating in a pendant and his features are aquiline, with the deformed Mayan nose, rather than Negroid. But these are only details. The figures are so alike that the same master craftsman might have made them both.

Finally he reads the footnote. The piece is somewhat larger than his own. It belongs to a collector in Los Angeles.

He shuts the book on his index finger and for several minutes looks straight ahead with a thoughtful expression. Mrs. Soquel promised that for thirty dollars it was a bargain and nobody with half an eye could dispute the fact. Yes. Yes, he reflects. I thought it must be good. As ignorant as I am of pre-Columbian art I had an idea it was excellent, which is why I bought it. Then the question of authenticity came up. Now we seem to have a third dimension—money. Not Mrs. Soquel's estimate but the actual market value. Thirty dollars. Hah! Thirty dollars indeed!

The woman in front of him moves uneasily and it occurs to Muhlbach that he must have spoken aloud.

He pops an olive into his mouth and studies the picture on the dust jacket of the book: a carved stone head wearing some sort of football helmet. This is the head of an Olmec. But just who or what is an Olmec?

He learns that *Olméca,* a word of Aztec origin, refers to those from the land of rubber. That is, inhabitants of the southern Gulf Coast with its *chico zapate* trees which provide the raw material for chewing gum. Here lived these enigmatic people— at La Venta, at Tres Zapotes, at San Lorenzo Tenochtitlán. In pestilential mangrove swamps twelve colossal basalt heads were found, dating from the fifth century before Christ, which the English sculptor Henry Moore described as the greatest works in spirit and form that he knew.

So far nobody has been able to find out where the Olmecs came from. But wherever Olmec artifacts turn up they are noticeably different from artifacts of the preclassic period. The stylistic discipline and the sculptural innovations provide evidence of a new religious concept and of a self-assured priesthood. Among the achievements of these mysterious people were the development of a scientific calendar and a system of writing. The so-called 'Mother Culture' of Mexico, Olmec artistic and theological ideas were to exert a profound and still discernible effect upon hundreds of millions.

Muhlbach stops reading long enough to look at another picture: one of the Tres Zapotes heads resting on its side, the broad Negroid nose not quite touching the earth. Beside the head squats a Mexican laborer whose fists might be large enough to plug the orifice of the nostrils. The stone lips are wider than the man's shoulders. There is something menacing and horrible about this ancient helmeted head in the abandoned field.

He continues turning the pages of this cabalistic book. Nayarit. Jalisco. Mixtec. Colima. Las Remojadas. Tlapacoya. El Tajín. Pánuco I, II and so forth from 1000 B.C. all the way to Pánuco VI and the Aztec conquest. Furthermore, to judge by the table of contents, that's hardly a start. Apparently one could spend a lifetime studying pre-Columbian civilizations.

He remembers the archaeology book his grandfather gave him and wonders what became of it. More important, what became of that first ambition? Strange, so many years later to rediscover the past.

He empties the martini and leans his forehead against the window. Not much to be seen. A few clouds, moonlight on the interminable midwestern fields. A river angling down. God knows which river. The Arkansas, maybe. Or the Platte or the Missouri. From six miles up what's the difference?

He watches the river approach. The sinuosity of its course begins to remind him of his own life. Like the river, he had assumed that he must be proceeding directly and forcefully toward his goal—whatever that goal happened to be. Not so. Just look at the deviations.

Again he is interrupted by the stewardess.

Supper.

He regards his yellow plastic tray with distaste. The utensils, too, are plastic, even the knife and fork. When he attempts to saw through the pressed chicken the knife bends like a toy. He considers picking up the wretched concoction and going after it with his teeth. New York is three hours away and one either eats this ersatz chicken freckled with coconut or one doesn't eat.

He pokes at the other delicacies. A warm roll accompanied by a square of butter stuck to a slip of waxed paper. A salad. Ah yes, the salad. Lettuce, beets, garbanzo beans, parsley and a slice of hardboiled egg submerged in orange toothpaste. Then there are the vegetables, which look oddly like models for an advertisement. He decides not to disturb them, the photographer should be along any minute. And the immaculate packaged condiments meant for a dollhouse. And a chocolate cupcake.

He eats the cupcake.

Behind the salad he discovers a sugary green mint in a cellophane envelope. Coffee has not yet arrived so he eats the mint while gazing soberly at the chicken. The chicken somehow manages to look defiant.

The stewardess has paused in the aisle. He glances up, expecting to see a pot of coffee. But instead of the stewardess he finds a dejected little person in a badly tailored department store suit with a sport shirt open at the neck—its flowery collar spreading across the lapels of the suit like tropical fungus. Whoever or whatever this individual is, the gods have not been kind. He is not a winner. A forked red beard gives him a Mephistophelean appearance, yet even at this he has not quite been successful. The points of his beard don't match.

Hello, he murmurs, gripping the top of the seat with a hand like a lobster's claw.

Muhlbach notes that his fingernails are dirty. No, not just dirty. Filthy.

The stranger, peering through eyeglasses as thick as binoculars, obviously hopes for an invitation to sit down. There is something gentle and appealing about him, but what does he want?

My name is Holmgren, he adds softly. He gestures at the book. I see you're into pre-Columbian. I'm into baskets, he continues, gaining strength by the moment. I'm so far into baskets my wife is about to leave me.

Baskets? Did you say 'baskets'?

Holmgren immediately sits down. For several seconds he stares straight ahead as though waiting to be evicted. When nothing happens he offers a timid smile.

I guess I didn't catch your name.

Muhlbach introduces himself. And then, as he feared, Holmgren wants to shake hands. Although there are many repulsive things in the world a set of grubby fingernails must be among the most offensive. Furthermore, Holmgren gives off a faint odor of tuna. The odor is unpleasant, but it is also curious because tuna was not on the menu. In any event, Holmgren's disgusting hand has been extended and there is no escape short of boorishness. Muhlbach clasps it.

During that brief, excruciating consummation the word 'Fate' comes to mind. Everything started in Mrs. Soquel's shop. Where will it end?

Did you board at Albuquerque? I don't recall seeing you.

I got on at Los Angeles.

Yes, Muhlbach thinks. Of course. Southern California is stamped all over him.

What takes you to New York, Mr. Holmgren?

I live there. I teach classical guitar at Roosevelt Junior College.

Muhlbach cannot prevent himself from looking again at the awful hands. The nails have not been clipped for so long that they are beginning to curl.

Holmgren scratches his scalp. He sucks his teeth. He crosses his legs. Evidently he plans to stay a while.

What got you into pre-Columbian?

Muhlbach explains about visiting Taos and buying the Mayan figure, adding that it was guaranteed. Then he goes on to tell about showing it to Quimby. He repeats what Quimby said, and mentions that not only did he get the Dockstader book but another one, beautifully illustrated, which he has not yet had a chance to read.

Holmgren, tugging his beard, listens gravely.

You got the piece with you?

Muhlbach opens the cigar box and takes out the Mayan just as the stewardess comes by to pick up the tray.

My! How unusual! What is that?

He explains, but again finds himself unable to stop. He points out to the stewardess the vestiges of the blue paint, the broken spikes, the scarification on the cheeks, the erosion of the surface caused by centuries of burial and even the beeswax.

My goodness! she answers. I think it's wonderful when you have an appreciation for art. My brother doesn't graduate from college until next June but he's already been offered a job.

Muhlbach, after thinking this over, decides he must have missed the connection.

Your brother is studying art?

Art? Oh no. He's going into electronics. This firm in Burbank has a simply fabulous retirement plan.

I see. Well, that sounds like a splendid opportunity.

Yes. Norbert's delighted. He'll be able to ride his motorcycle every weekend. Can I get you some more coffee?

Bring us a drink, Holmgren says boldly. What'll you have, Muhlbach? I'm paying.

I don't understand a word of this, Muhlbach thinks. None of this makes any sense.

Manhattan. Two cherries. Right?

No. A martini with two olives.

Look, pal, says Holmgren, tapping Muhlbach on the arm. If that guy told you he had no doubts about the piece that means it's good because as a rule they give you nothing but doubletalk. Know what I mean? They're afraid to commit themselves, see, because their reputation is at stake. For instance, suppose they call a piece good but it turns out to be bad. What happens? They're disgraced. Everybody finds out. They lose face just like Orientals. They're worried about losing face, take my word for it. Of course with baskets this is not the problem because they don't fake baskets—not as much any-how.

He wants to talk about baskets. That's the reason he sat down, Muhlbach thinks. He doesn't care about pre-Columbian. He just wants to talk about baskets.

You know what? Holmgren continues with an air of triumphant confidence. My wife and I went to this auction because she needed a throw rug for the game room, see, and there was this basket. It went for a hundred bucks. A hundred smackers! I said to my wife—I said 'Honey, anybody who'd pay a hundred for a wicker basket has got to be loose in the head.' That's what I told her. But you know who was loose in the head?

Holmgren pauses long enough to tap himself significantly.

It was a Pomo feathered, mint condition. Natur-ally I didn't know that at the time because I didn't know thing one about baskets but I remember what it looked like. A Pomo feathered, top quality, for a measly hundred and I said to my wife the guy must be nuts. Would you believe it?

Holmgren is now fairly launched. He discusses his collection in stupefying detail. He has a pair of matched Pitt River that anybody would love to own. He has what might be one of the oldest Maidu storage baskets in existence—not in very good shape, naturally. One of his treasures is a Chemehuevi—he's never seen another like it. And he has a Papago yucca fiber split-stitch over a foundation of bear grass.

He pauses to let this news penetrate.

Is that so? Muhlbach replies. Well, your collection must be valuable.

Holmgren, tugging his beard, smiles modestly. Then he goes on. He has more than seventy bas-kets—Klikitat, Nootka, Pima, Tulare, Panamint, mostly West Coast but a few Eastern Woodland. He has a little gem of a Pomo with abalone pendants. Nothing like the one that got away, mind you. It shows some wear, but a first-rate item just the same.

Listen, pal, he says with a wink, you stand Brigitte Bardot next to a museum quality Tlingit and I wouldn't see her. I got a real nice Tlingit, by the way, got it at auction for eighteen bucks. A steal. It's worth a lot more. Pretty scarce. And talk about scarce—listen, a friend of mine got a Washo by Datsolali. When he said Datsolali I just laughed. But it's a fact. They tell him it's 1910, maybe earlier, only they won't certify it. Like I said, they're afraid to lose face.

Why does he ramble on like this? Muhlbach wonders. He must realize I have no interest in baskets, although I'd like to find out about those auctions. They auction office equipment and farm machinery and French impressionist paintings and cattle and horses and unclaimed trunks, but apparently old wicker baskets also go on the block. That's worth remembering. It might be possible to pick up some pre-Columbian. I'd love another Jaina. Or a Nayarit warrior. Or one of those delightful pre-classic Chupícuaro ladies.

The stewardess reappears. Would they care to purchase earphones for the movie which will start in a few minutes?

Holmgren is annoyed. No. No earphones. He wants to go on discussing baskets.

Muhlbach interrupts before he can get back to the Nootkas and Klikitats.

These auctions, Holmgren. I'd like to know more.

So he learns about Wes Piglett from Arcadia, which is a suburb of Los Angeles. John Wesley Piglett, named in honor of the notorious outlaw John Wesley Hardin. Wes is an auctioneer of ethnographic items. He travels around the country buying private collections, buying blankets and weapons and fetishes and jewelry from Indians, buying Mexican and Central American pre-Columbian items from runners—Muhlbach blinks at the word. That was Mrs. Soquel's term for smugglers.

Wes buys from everybody, but he gets most of his stock from dealers going out of business. He buys anything. Baskets, rugs, pistols, Winchesters, spurs, peace pipes, Chevron trade beads, cradle boards, elk teeth, pestles, squash blossom necklaces, Clovis points, branding irons, old silver dollars, fossils, gorgets, bull roarers—you name it.

Pre-Columbian, you say? What sort?

Pots, effigies, carvings. Holmgren becomes vague. Pre-Columbian isn't his thing.

Where does Piglett hold these auctions?

Holmgren scratches his neck with one abominable fingernail before answering.

L.A. Frisco. Dallas. St. Louis. New York. Wes covers about a dozen cities. He used to work only the Coast and Arizona but so many people are getting into ethnography that he's expanded. And the prices, man, the prices! You won't believe me but it's the truth. Straight up. Three years ago I could have got a really rare Yakima beadwork for peanuts. Today? Out of sight. Everything's up and going higher. Not just baskets. Fetishes, silverwork, turquoise. Needlepoint turquoise, for instance. Dealers estimate it's going up thirty per cent a year. At least. Beautiful stuff, granted. Top grade, good color, and they grind it so small you'd swear it would break.

Who is 'they'?

Zuñi. Nobody else makes needlepoint. Navajo work is heavier. Or pottery. Now you take Maria. I was talking to this dealer who bought a red Maria—not a black, mind you, but a red—just a few years ago for thirty-five bucks. What was he offered last year? You won't believe me. You'll call me a liar. Nine hundred! Out of sight. Next year it'll be worse. I should have bought that Yakima.

You say this Piglett fellow gets to New York?

He'll be in Queens the twentieth of February.

Queens? Why Queens?

Holmgren shrugs. How should I know? Seagrave's Hi-Way House. February twentieth. I hope I can make it.

Muhlbach looks at him suspiciously. The entire business has begun to sound rather odd. Seagrave's is a prominent luxury motel. Nevertheless, what kind of an auctioneer works out of motels? And this nearsighted guitar-playing basket collector with the resplendent sport shirt and rotting fingernails— is he authentic, so to speak, or could he be a hustler for John Wesley Piglett? If he does teach at Roosevelt what is he doing on this plane? He doesn't look much like a touring concert guitarist. He doesn't look as if he could raise five dollars. Strange. Very strange.

I gather that you and Piglett are fairly well acquainted.

But Holmgren perceives a deeper question:

You want to know if Wes can be trusted. Listen, Muhlbach, you've been around. I don't need to tell you to look both ways when you cross the street. I'm not saying Wes is crooked, understand? Those ancient cultures need a lot of study. Hell, even the museums get a bad piece now and then. You follow me?

Enough to know I'd better be careful, Muhlbach thinks. I have no idea what this bird is up to, but I'd better watch out. It might be entertaining to go to that auction, but if I do I certainly won't bid on anything. This has all the marks of a shell game.

And while the movie is playing he considers what Holmgren has said. Actors flicker on and off the screen mouthing inaudible lines and it occurs to him that their behavior is singularly appropriate. An experienced lip reader could follow them as easily as a connoisseur could distinguish a fake from the genuine article. But an amateur—well, he reminds himself, if I do attend that auction I'll be smart. I won't forget my ignorance.

The seat belt sign blinks.

A moment later the Captain delivers the customary speech. We are beginning our descent into the greater New York area. On behalf of the crew and myself may I say that it has been a pleasure having you aboard—and blah-blah. But what is the Captain actually thinking? Or perhaps the speech was prerecorded. The jet howls lower and closer to its destination while the Captain, whose hobby is collecting early American firearms, discusses this fascinating subject with the copilot, whose passion is Navajo blankets.

In the terminal as he waits and waits and waits beside the conveyor belt, Muhlbach again considers the idea of going to Piglett's auction. He decides it would be foolish.

Suitcases, hatboxes, duffel bags, canisters of film, sports equipment and various other objects pop through the hatch, slide down the turntable and begin circling the metal cone. But not the one article that counts. They've lost it. This time they've lost it.

At last, though, as always, the machinery spews up his suitcase with a few fresh scratches to prove that the trip was not a dream. And Muhlbach, his homburg settled against the January night, firmly carrying his possessions, strides through the automatic doors to capture a taxi.

Yes, I've decided, he thinks while hurtling along the expressway with disaster an instant beyond the windshield. I won't go. It pays to be cautious. I'll be sensible. If I want to get involved in this pre-Columbian nonsense—and I'm not at all sure I do—

I'll go to a reputable gallery. I've learned just enough to realize I could get stung. I am not knowledgeable enough to be hunting bargains at an auction, certainly not at a motel auction operated by some California suede shoe artist named Piglett. Look both ways when you cross the street. Good advice. All right, that's that.

But even as he tells himself these things he knows he will be at Seagrave's Hi-Way House on the twentieth.

Snow is falling. He looks out the window of the taxi at the inconstant lights of New York and imagines himself in Taos. Is it snowing there? Is the plaza empty? Have those Indians moved? And where would Mrs. Soquel be right now? Half past midnight, so it's ten-thirty in New Mexico. Maybe she and her sister have gone to the inn for a drink in front of that adobe fireplace. No, probably not. Chances are they've already gone to bed. Ten-thirty in the mountains would seem very late.

I wonder if I could live there, he whispers. Why not? Yesterday the question would have made me laugh. But of course I can't move to New Mexico. Impossible.

What about the children? What would a metropolitan child make of a place like that? Those plateaus can be terrifying. Mountains unraveling all the way to Colorado—growing up in the presence of such a phenomenon, how would that affect a child? Or those translucent mornings sharp as an icicle—how different from the boisterous urgency of New York.

Then there's Mrs. Grunthe. New Mexico would drive her mad with frustration. She'd need a completely new set of enemies. Imagine Mrs. Grunthe elbowing the citizens of Taos aside as she plods toward the market. That rancher, for instance. What a confrontation. Incredible. No, she belongs where she is. The one thing in life she enjoys is haranguing the neighborhood butcher. The chops, the chicken, the hamburger, the roast—even the best meat isn't satisfactory. New Yorkers grow accustomed to eccentrics but what Taos butcher would put up with her complaints?

Otto wouldn't like it either. Donna might, but he wouldn't. Nothing stimulates him these days except hockey. And next summer a new baseball season just like the last, God save us. Suggest leaving the Rangers and Mets and Jets and whatever other Philistines we support. Try it. Suggest that only once and listen to the melody of outraged disbelief.

As for Donna, yes, she might go along. In fact she'd probably love the idea. She's too young for New York to have acquired much meaning but she's mad about horses. She could be bribed. Donna, we might even get a horse. Yes, that one remark should be enough. Her dresser is a ceramic horseshow. They all look alike with their stereotyped poses and dreadful cream glaze, but she can tell them apart. And what a day when Mrs. Grunthe knocked one over while dusting. Useless to point out that it could be replaced for approximately forty-nine cents. Grief can't be assuaged by logic. That was not just any horse—that was Prince shattered on the hardwood floor.

Then it occurs to Muhlbach that his daughter might be called a connoisseur of these dimestore animals. The thought is a little discomfiting. What distinguishes one clay bibelot from another? The Mayan may be five hundred years old, true, and somewhat less common than a manufactured palomino, nevertheless the similarity is embarrassing.

He remembers that his grandfather admired the paintings of Burne-Jones, manifestly an absurd judgment. And yet, he reflects, my grandfather was sensitive, educated and intelligent. So it seems to be a matter of taste. Consequently, who's to decide whether a gimcrack horse is a lesser or greater work of art than a Mayan lord steeped in the centuries. But still, I'm right. Donna is a child. Her taste is childish. Soon enough her collection will find its way to the attic and from there to a Salvation Army shop. My grandfather's taste, though—what could account for that? Well, there must be standards. Maybe it depends on one's schooling. I suppose I could find out. At least I could investigate the business. I could pick up a book on aesthetics by some properly accredited mandarin. Burne-Jones rather than Rembrandt. Extraordinary. There's got to be an explanation. I recall hearing about an Oriental musician who visited Europe and could scarcely keep from laughing at a Bruckner symphony. How is it possible?

The problem follows him halfway home from the airport. Then he reminds himself that already he has wasted much too much time in the never-never land of Art. The purpose of the trip was to evaluate Occidental Life and tomorrow the directors will pick his brains. Tell us, Muhlbach, what about the feasibility of merger? We are gathered at this expensive table not to hear your impressions of January in Taos but to debate certain proposals entailing substantial sums of—excuse the expression—Money! We didn't send you West to indulge yourself in vague artistic rumination. Now, concerning Occidental, let us hear what you have to say.

He frowns. Those hours on the plane wasted. Instead of putting my notes in order, what did I do? Looked at pictures and listened to some imbecile talk about baskets.

Once inside the house he snaps on the light in the hall and stands for a moment listening. Not a sound.

Carefully he walks upstairs, avoiding the step

that squeaks, enters the master bedroom and sets down his suitcase. Then, still wearing his hat and coat, he walks to the door of the children's room and listens again. They must be asleep.

With one gloved hand he turns the knob and opens the door enough to peek in.

Otto is sleeping as though Mrs. Grunthe has at last succumbed to temptation and hit him with a club. How odd that barely audible noises—a dog barking half a mile away, perhaps a mouse running across the floor—sometimes will wake him up while at other times he would sleep through the explosion of Krakatoa. His hockey stick, the handle reinforced with electrician's tape, has fallen to the carpet beside the bed. No doubt he was pretending to be a star of the Rangers when sleep surprised him.

Muhlbach, looking down somberly at the boyish face which is his own yet not his own, realizes that he can feel four distinct emotions. They are as simple to identify as the primary colors of the patchwork quilt on Otto's bed: affection, jealousy, love and exasperation. Not a particularly harmonious blend.

But to define what he feels as he looks at his daughter asleep—that's difficult. Maybe I don't want to know, he thinks. Why analyze it?

So he stands outside the door watching her without comprehension, and holds his breath because it seems to him that if he looks long enough—well, who can guess what might happen? Perhaps a dozen fairies will alight and begin dancing in a ring on her pillow.

Suddenly Donna coughs. What a small cough. She didn't even move.

He shuts the door without a sound.

As he walks past Mrs. Grunthe's room he doesn't stop. The very idea of looking in on Mrs. Grunthe is monstrous. She's there, all right, as substantially asleep as a plow horse. A monotonous buzz can be heard. Is she dreaming? Mrs. Grunthe, what do you dream about? What lugubrious Nordic thoughts prance through your head?

Dream, sir? Dream, did you say? Why should a sensible person waste these blessed hours of rest dreaming?

Praise be to Mrs. Grunthe. Without that indestructible surrogate what would become of the children? —now that their mother's gone. Amen, Muhlbach murmurs, closing the door of his own room. Have a good rest, Mrs. Grunthe.

He starts to unpack. It's a tedious process. Why should unpacking be more tiresome than packing? Just the same, it is. Comb and brush. Razor. Deodorant. Toothbrush and toothpaste. Shirts. Underwear. Neckties. Handkerchiefs. Socks. Then he finds a roll of peppermints he bought in Denver and an implacable urge to leave New York sweeps through him. Get your hockey stick, Otto, we're moving. Donna, collect your ceramic thoroughbreds. Mrs. Grunthe, kiss the butcher goodby. We're off to the Wild West. We're off to Colorado or New Mexico or some such place where it's so quiet you can hear the icicles melt.

For a few minutes he sits on the bed sucking a peppermint and remembering the frozen earth, the altitude, the odd sense of vacancy, the perpetual silence. How unreal it seems.

A glance at the pre-Columbian art books and the cigar box confirms the trip. Yes, it was real. Denver and Albuquerque and Taos and Mrs. Soquel and Quimby.

He pulls the red rubber band from the box with a feeling of apprehension and lifts the lid.

As expected, the Mayan is lying rigidly on his

back but again he seems to have worked his way
upward through the excelsior as though he resented
the indignity:

I am a lord of the realm! By whose authority do
you confine me?

Pushing aside the last few strands of excelsior
Muhlbach gazes at the irascible homunculus—at
this compressed embodiment of life, vehement and
absolute.

The Mayan stares right through him.

Well, after you've heard the storms and revolu-
tions of centuries why notice your present custodian?
Which is exactly what I am, he reflects. To pretend
that I 'bought' this statue or that I 'own' it is a
conceit. Set the two of us side by side and there
wouldn't be much doubt about who owns whom. I
have a temporary responsibility, that's all. In twenty
or thirty years some other innocent will take up my
duties. Probably Otto—he should be the next custodian. But maybe not. Not unless he outgrows the
Rangers. I wouldn't entrust this to a hockey player.
So we'll wait and see. It depends, too, on the sort
of woman Donna becomes.

Meanwhile, my friend, he continues, balancing
the Mayan on his palm, where would you like to
sit for the next few decades?

OTTO, Donna and Mrs. Grunthe receive their first lesson in pre-Columbian art the following night after supper. From the green leather depths of his favorite armchair Muhlbach presides, holding both books on his lap because he intends to illustrate the lecture with pictures.

From a place of honor on the mantel the Mayan looks above their heads into a tremendous and indecipherable past.

Well now, he begins, and observes with satisfaction that his three students are waiting respectfully. Well, the fact of the matter is that our knowledge of early American civilization is woefully incomplete. Just the same we can learn quite a lot about the way these people used to live if we study their art objects. Not only how they dressed and what their musical instruments and ceremonial paraphernalia looked like, but to some extent we can even deduce the sorts of games they played and the nature of their religious beliefs, the influence of neighboring groups or 'tribes,' and so forth. In any case, the earliest examples of representational art—by which I mean animals or birds or people or any object recognizable as such—these were discovered at Tlatilco and El Arbolillo and Zacatenco. I realize the names don't mean anything, but we'll get back to them after a while. First, you might like to know how these little figures were made. The artist took a lump of clay which he modeled with his fingers and sometimes with a stick. Then he polished it with a smooth stone and next he baked it in an oven the way Mrs. Grunthe bakes cookies.

Otto and Donna thereupon look at Mrs. Grunthe, who purses her lips because of so much attention.

Otto turns abruptly toward the statue, perhaps to see if it resembles a cookie. Donna yawns. Mrs. Grunthe shoots a determined glance at the kitchen.

Muhlbach decides to speed up his lecture.

Listen, everybody. A great many years ago—even before Jesus was born—these Mexican Indians were fishing and farming and living together in communities which later became important cities with big beautiful pyramids like those in Egypt, such as Chichén Itzá and Teotihuacán.

He opens one of the books to show a colored photograph of a merchant from Teotihuacán.

This was painted on the wall of a priest's apartment sometime during the fifth or sixth century. Those ancient Indians had gods and priests the same as we do.

Mrs. Grunthe's eye immediately pins him to the chair.

Their priests were different from ours, of course. They believed very different things. It's just that the people regarded them as priests.

She seems mollified by this. Her granite expression softens a little.

Now, everybody. Look at the man in this painting. Do you see him? He's carrying weapons and a shield because he was a salesman who had to travel through dangerous country a long way from home. See the weapons?

Mrs. Grunthe and Otto dutifully look at the picture but Donna is someplace else. She has pulled off her shoes and is lying on her stomach in front of the fireplace. In a few minutes she will be asleep.

Muhlbach shuts the book. What's the use of going any further? Nobody cares.

Otto, surprisingly, claims he would like to know more about the statue.

Muhlbach studies him. No, he's faking. He's as bored as the other two. Yet pre-Columbian art is so unfamiliar, so complex, so rich with overtones— how could anybody, even a child, be bored?

Mr. Quimby has promised to do some research and will write to me. When I hear from him I'll let you know what he found out.

Okay. I'm going to go work on my plane.

For the last month Otto has been assembling a plastic Messerschmitt. Once upon a time it took forever to build a model plane, but these days everything is pre-formed. The 'work' seems to consist of sticking on swastikas.

How's it coming along?

Okay, I guess.

And now Mrs. Grunthe is up. She asks what time he would like to be called in the morning, although she knows perfectly well. It's just that something should be said before walking out.

Oh, the usual time. Incidentally, that pot roast was delicious. Absolutely delicious, Mrs. Grunthe. Your cooking gets better and better.

She responds as expected, by denigrating the butcher. But it pays to keep her well supplied with compliments, otherwise she takes revenge by serving macaroni casserole. Chicken à la king. Irish stew. Chipped beef.

Then for a long time after his students have disappeared Muhlbach sits in the armchair reading.

The following night when he comes home he finds a gift, which Mrs. Grunthe has placed in a pie pan because it seems to be leaking some kind of sugary fluid. Wrapped in tinfoil like a mummy, emitting a powerful odor of rum, it is presumably a fruitcake. But from whom? And why?

The gift is from Miss Cunningham.

And Mrs. Grunthe is not reluctant to add that in her opinion this fruitcake would kill anybody who ate it.

Muhlbach, a trifle dizzy from the fumes, tentatively peels away the tinfoil. Slices of fruit, metamorphosed into red and blue and green sugar crystals by Eula's culinary magic, glisten with poisonous promise. Mrs. Grunthe is probably right, it would be dangerous to eat this. The last time Eula displayed her skill she produced a bag of ginger cookies hard enough to split the teeth of a squirrel. Otto ate them, claiming they were good. He would eat this fruitcake, too, if he got the chance.

Ah hah! Muhlbach exclaims, backing away. Now that was thoughtful of her.

Hmmph, replies Mrs. Grunthe. And what shall I do with it? Will you tell me that, sir?

Oh, let's see. Suppose we just put it someplace.

Are you planning to call Miss Cunningham?

Yes, of course. I'll give her a ring in a day or so.

And what if she telephones tomorrow with you at the office? What am I to say?

Why, you can say I appreciate the gift. It was very nice of her.

Mrs. Grunthe, muttering, walks off with Eula's chef-d'oeuvre and Muhlbach sits down to consider the situation. Eula has entered her domestic phase again. Well, the best thing is to ignore it. She recovers from these misadventures as though nothing had happened, the way other women recover from fainting spells.

But I mustn't forget to thank her, he reminds himself. Tomorrow maybe, or the day after. That should be soon enough.

Monday evening when he gets home he finds a

postcard from Quimby, and realizes that he had been anticipating a letter—a three-page or four-page letter not only specifying the provenance but filled with details such as the probable site from which the statue was taken and perhaps speculation about the identity of the priest or king it represents.

Well, if Quimby's report is brief, at least it's prompt. He writes that the figure could be from the state of Chiapas. Style of headdress and scarification of the cheeks indicate a date no earlier than the eighth or ninth century and possibly as late as the thirteenth. He concludes on a personal note:

'A majority of these little pieces are broken so you are fortunate to have one intact.'

Muhlbach immediately writes to thank him for the information.

However, both books assign such figures to the classic period which ended in the tenth century. Nor does either book mention them being made or excavated in Chiapas.

I should have had the courage to point that out, he thinks. We might have developed a worthwhile correspondence, now it's too late. I wonder if he's wrong about the thirteenth century. And where did he get that notion about Chiapas? I suspect he may have dug it out of a library. All right, I can do the same and we'll just see what we'll see.

Alsberg. Anders, Anton. Ashton. Batres. Bernal. Brainerd. Burland. Caso. Coe. Covarrubias. There's hardly a shortage of authorities, but which would be suitable for the ambitious beginner? Quimby mentioned Coe, so he ought to be a good bet. Who else? Collier. Corona. Delgado. Disselhoff. Emmerich. And so forth all the way down to *Die Hieroglyphen der Mayahandschriften* by Günther Zimmermann.

Muhlbach returns from another day at the office with three more books in his briefcase.

He learns that some Jaina miniatures were

molded. Others, such as his own, were entirely hand-made. With others a technique called *pastillaje* was employed, in which the factory-made figures were hand-decorated with strips and pellets of wet clay. After they had dried in the sun they were painted and the brilliant color was preserved by firing at a low temperature, sacrificing durability for aesthetic effect, which explains why so many of the pieces are broken. Ah ha! This coincides with Quimby's remark.

Very similar in style to Jaina ceramics are the Nopiloa Mayoid figures—so similar that at first they were thought to be imports into southern Veracruz, although recent evidence has established their origin in the lower Rio Blanco—Papaloapan region. Nopiloa figures invariably are hollow and usually they are either rattles or whistles, or both. The walls of these pieces are exceptionally thin, made of a fine clay without temper which fires from reddish orange to gray with a predominant . . .

Muhlbach stops reading. The clock in the hall has begun to chime. He counts the hours, expecting ten. But eleven strikes, and then twelve. He frowns. It's ridiculous to stay up so late, considering tomorrow's schedule. However, this is a particularly instructive chapter.

And not a great many more chapters have passed before he feels competent to discuss the stylistic differences between Nayarit Chinesco, say, and Jalisco El Arenal Brown—if anybody should ask. Or the distinguishing characteristics of Tres Zapotes II, or Monte Albán III. Not that anybody will ask. Not Mrs. Grunthe, Otto or Donna. Nobody at the office. In fact he does not know anybody who has even the slightest understanding of pre-Columbian art.

Wednesday night, settled in his armchair with a good fire going and a snifter of brandy on the table,

six chapters into *Ancient Arts of the Americas,*
he looks up with mild annoyance when Mrs.
Grunthe enters.

Yes?

Miss Cunning . . .

But Eula has not merely arrived, already she is
in the room taking off her cloak and talking:

Now don't try to apologize because I won't believe a word—not a single word! I do think you
might have called. Really, I shouldn't be speaking
to you! Oh, you're impossible! And you've been
away. Where on earth were you?

Muhlbach, getting to his feet, replies that he has
been on a business trip. And I'm sorry, Eula. I do
appreciate the fruitcake. I'm afraid I've neglected
my social obligations.

You certainly have! I want you to know I'm absolutely furious. Now I'm going to stay only a
moment, so you can relax. I wouldn't for the world
interrupt whatever you're doing but as you may or
may not know there's a perfect blizzard outside. May
I have some tea?

Yes, of course. I was about to say that I intended
to call you over the weekend.

Then why didn't you?

He picks up the book.

I've gotten very much interested in pre-Columbian
art. This picture on the cover, for example, is a
classic Mochica portrait vase dating from the first
few centuries A.D.—perhaps fourth to seventh—
which establishes it as more or less contemporary
with early Tiahuanaco. It's from the north coast of
Peru not far from Cajamarca. You'll observe that
it still has quite a bit of the original paint.

Eula, clasping her hands, looks at the picture with
unmistakable distaste.

But once again Muhlbach finds himself unable to
stop. On and on he goes, describing the characteris-

tics of Mochica pottery, turning the pages of his book, reading especially informative passages, comparing drawings with photographs, correlating everything with references to the chronological charts and maps of archaeological sites.

Eula, sipping tea, plucks at her beads in silent despair.

From time to time while he reads and expounds he glances at her. Obviously she is bored. Yet it seems to him that before long she will begin to listen.

He displays a photograph of a burnished black spout-and-bridge vessel representing a jaguar. The markings are incised. The surface must have been covered at one time with resinous post-fired colors. From the south coast of Peru. Formative period. Paracas style. Isn't it incredible?

Eula responds that she is glad he has a new hobby.

After thinking about this remark Muhlbach shuts the book. Pre-Columbian art is too important to be called a hobby. Gardening is a hobby. Stamp collecting is a hobby. Chasing butterflies. Decorating lampshades. How could anybody compare such trivial exercises with the study of pre-Columbian art? But it's my own fault, he reflects. It was stupid of me to try to force this on her. She likes those little bisque figurines in department stores. Royal Doulton poodles balancing on their hind legs.

Eula looks out the window and is relieved to discover that the snow has almost stopped. She sets aside her tea cup.

I suppose I'll forgive you this one time! But you must must call me. Do you hear?

Yes. I promise I will. We might take in a show one of these evenings.

Marvelous! I haven't seen you in ages, dear boy. Au revoir!

And she vanishes, leaving rather too much perfume as a memento of her visit. She also contrives to leave behind an eyebrow pencil which, naturally, must be returned before long.

Muhlbach, sinking into his chair, reaches for the brandy. Eula is exhausting. Why? Because of those superlatives? Wonderful! Furious! Marvelous! She can't seem to express anything moderately. She charges the atmosphere with a kind of madness—maybe the result of desperation, some sense of loneliness. God knows. And she certainly has been putting on weight. But I should have called, he tells himself severely. And I will. Leaving the eyebrow pencil was absurd. Women can be so obvious, especially when they think they're being subtle. But I must give her a call. We could go to the ballet or something.

However, Eula's eyebrow pencil has not yet been returned when February suddenly appears on the calendar.

Perhaps stimulated by the new moon, she calls. On the telephone her sugary voice feigns distress:

I'm just so put out with you! After all those promises!

I've been preoccupied, Eula. I'm sorry. I seem to spend every night reading.

I accept your apology. I shouldn't, but I will. Isn't that gracious of me? Now listen, you bad boy. My dear dear friend Prissy Bippus—have you met Prissy? I'm so forgetful. Anyway, Prissy has just returned from a round-the-world junket with her fourth husband, Dr. David Ascher. You haven't met David, I'm sure, so you see I've not completely lost my senses. Now where was I? Oh! David is an eye surgeon and quite well thought of, from what I'm told, though frightfully expensive.

Yes yes yes, he thinks. Come to the point, Eula.

Well, according to Prissy they squandered a king's

ransom on art treasures in the Orient. David, as you might suspect, is a very highly regarded connoisseur. By the way, you two did meet, did you not?

We did not, he replies more irritably than he intended.

I thought you had. Although it doesn't matter. What I was about to say was that David has what literally amounts to a private museum. Imagine! I'm dying to see his collection, aren't you? And Prissy says they're having a small 'do' a week from Friday—not elaborate. I know you despise large gatherings.

So that's why she called. She needs an escort. All right, why doesn't she say so? Why can't she come right out and invite me?

While she continues circling the topic like a matronly butterfly wondering how and where to alight, he thinks it over. Eula talks too much, much too much, and sometimes gets hysterical. On the other hand, she's lively and affectionate and despite the cascade of words an evening with her is never dull. Besides, Dr. Ascher may have catholic tastes. He might have some pre-Columbian artifacts tucked in among the netsukes.

At last Eula pops the question: Would you care to accompany me?

Yes, I would. Very much.

Are you sure?

Of course.

I was positive you'd refuse.

Not at all. I'll be looking forward to it. Now tell me, does this Dr. Ascher collect anything except Oriental art?

I haven't the foggiest notion. But you must promise not to say a word about those ghastly idols.

Not unless Ascher brings it up. What time?

Eight o'clock. You won't forget?

I'm making a note right now. Eight o'clock week from Friday.

Wonderful! You'll adore Prissy. Goodnight! Sweet dreams!

Goodnight, Eula.

'Ghastly idols,' he remarks aloud after hanging up the telephone. However, it's foolish to feel offended. Eula is no more capable of appreciating pre-Columbian art than Mrs. Grunthe. In fact, it would be easier to educate Otto. All right, no more proselytizing. As for the evening with David and Prissy—well, Ascher's collection might be a pleasant surprise. We'll see. As Holmgren would put the matter: Let's find out what he's into.

And during the next few days Muhlbach admits that he is indeed beginning to anticipate the Aschers' party. Even the idea of meeting Prissy. What sort of woman would run around with a name like that?

On the appointed Friday, dressed in a dark suit fresh from the cleaners, his shoes polished, his hat settled against the north wind and Eula's exotic souvenir in his breast pocket, he rings the bell at her apartment.

After a while he rings again.

This time she answers: Yes? Who's there, please?

For God's sake, Eula, who else would it be? Open the door. I'm freezing.

Once inside he pulls off his gloves in order to blow on his fingers, stamps his feet on the carpet for a while and then decides to walk up instead of waiting for the elevator.

Eula stands poised in her doorway, arms outstretched like a Wagnerian soprano. But instead of a kiss she goes twirling across the rug to display her new dress. Muhlbach, watching her pirouette, reflects that although it has not been very long since her visit she has managed to put on several pounds.

Nor is it the dress. No, it isn't an illusion, it's all Eula. Up to this point one could charitably have described her as delectable, enticing, ample, or by some other Victorian circumlocution. Not now. Fat is the word. Fat.

Her thick glossy auburn hair has been coiled and somehow encouraged to remain aloft. It may fall down or it may stay up. One can seldom predict what will happen with Eula. She glides across waxed floors as though she had been raised in a ballroom but then manages to trip over a thread.

And the dress, or costume, is one she herself has designed. It could be called vaguely Oriental. Brocaded silk with a tight high collar and voluminous sleeves. He thinks of Madame Chiang Kai-shek, although he cannot imagine why because there's not much resemblance, excepting the material. Eula makes most of her own clothing and it always has a peculiar unfinished look, as though at the last moment she had misplaced the pattern.

Do you like it? Now be honest.

Yes. Yes indeed. That's quite a creation, he adds, gazing at the dress with a determined expression which he hopes she will mistake for approval. The sleeves are fascinating. He visualizes Eula at supper majestically dipping her billowing sleeves in the soup.

Don't you adore it? I feel light as a bird!

Yes, it does look comfortable. Shall we go?

Oh, I despise you! You haven't said one nice thing. Let me take another peek in the mirror, then we'll be off.

Twenty minutes later they are on the way. However, Eula cannot seem to locate the Aschers' address.

Did you leave it in the apartment?

No, of course I didn't, silly. It's in my purse. For Heaven's sake, be patient.

He is about to suggest calling Prissy when Eula utters a scream of triumph:

Ooo! What a relief! I was so afraid I'd left it in the apartment.

Dr. Ascher and the former Prissy Bippus are only a shade less picturesque than Eula. Prissy is tall, taller than her husband, cadaverous and fashionably round-shouldered with the fatigued air of those who incessantly attend parties. She wears a black velvet jumpsuit with a chain of gold coins slung like a challenge across flat sexless hips. Octagonal steel glasses are in style this season, halfway down her nose so she can peer over them. Thousands of cocktails have done their work on her vocal cords. Prissy's voice could be filtered through a porch screen.

Husband number four, David, is a trim little fellow about fifty years old—alert, nimble, probably a handball player, intelligent and obviously conceited—with silky blue-rinsed hair and the peevish expression of a lap dog.

When they shake hands Muhlbach feels disturbed by the soft mindless grip, rather like that of a trained monkey. As soon as he can do so without being conspicuous he looks at the doctor's hands. They are fragile and neat, manicured, no larger than the hands of a woman. Ascher should be a good surgeon. Unquestionably he is successful. His suit is expensive and tailor-made. Except for the tinted hair he has taste. But I don't care for him, Muhlbach thinks. Although he might be worth talking to.

However there's not much chance for conversation. Guests are still streaming in. The so-called small gathering has grown to thirty or forty. Prissy slouches toward each arrival with emaciated fingers clutching, upper lip peeled back to illustrate her pleasure.

Eula talks and talks, enthusiastically transferring

her monologue from one guest to the next. Now and then she flies away to pounce on an old friend or a new friend. Or a stranger. The main thing, apparently, is to prevent silence. Well, all right. As the kids say, do your thing. Besides, her loquacity is useful. Muhlbach finds himself free to stroll through the house inspecting Bokhara rugs and lacquered furniture. He spends a while gazing at a flood-lighted terrace which must be overflowing with guests during the summer when the Aschers give a really big party. Surgeons do make money, but living on this scale suggests an inheritance.

The 'private museum' is not a figure of speech. On the far side of the terrace beyond the swimming pool stands a brutally modern glass and steel gallery, formidable as a prison.

Guests who wish to see the collection are given an escorted tour. Most of the guests already have seen it, so tonight the group will be small.

Ascher leads the way.

Eula, clinging warmly to Muhlbach's arm, whispers that they are in luck because Ascher himself doesn't very often conduct the tour. Usually he leaves it up to Prissy.

The gallery isn't large, and each object has been provided with so much display space that at first the effect is of emptiness, as though some of the pieces might be out on loan. But after a few minutes it becomes clear that nothing could be added without affecting the balance, nor has anything mediocre been included.

The first stop is a ceramic T'ang lady holding a mirror. No expertise is required to appreciate her limpid beauty. The sensitive oval face, the impertinent pointed slippers, the orange and green gown. Beneath a small spotlight she admires herself with unbearable grace. Yes, she is exquisite, Muhlbach thinks. No question about it.

Nearby, dominating an alcove, as masculine as the lady is feminine, a stolid iron head of Buddha confronts the guests. Larger than life, Buddha wears a peculiar helmet studded with hundreds of knobs which undoubtedly symbolize something—perhaps the eight hundred prescribed attitudes for meditation—although Dr. Ascher doesn't explain.

Next is a wooden temple dog. In a shrill nasal voice Ascher catalogues the age, provenance and style.

No. No, no, Muhlbach says to himself. The thing is excellent, of course. I can tell that. But it has no meaning.

This would be your typical late Han *po-shan hsiang-lu,* Ascher continues, turning toward a bronze censer inlaid with gold and rubies.

Eula claps her hands, speechless with admiration.

Muhlbach, bending down for a close look at the censer, reflects that she has probably decided to hold a few compliments in reserve. She has already exclaimed over the T'ang lady and the temple dog and it would be embarrassing to trot out the same adjectives time after time. The censer, though, is worth inspecting. Severely modeled, its form has been deliberately restricted in order to emphasize the value of the inlay. If I saved like a Spartan for twenty years, he thinks, I might manage the down payment. Not that I particularly want it.

As they move along he notices the baleful red light of an electric eye.

Ascher stops beside a dancing deity with fourteen arms and a pointed hat. This would be Cambodian. A trifle ornate, but a decent example. Twelfth century. One of my earliest acquisitions.

Eula finds it utterly fascinating.

I don't, Muhlbach comments to himself. It bores me. He looks around. Opposite the dancer stands a ponderous marble Buddha—or could it be a Bodhisattva?—missing two fingers, dressed in an ankle-length garment, overfed and complacent.

Ascher explains:

The evolution of these may be traced from the compact body and the pleated robe to the more elongated type executed with precise strokes. During the sixth century, as may be observed here, the style softens. The line becomes fluid. More sinuous. The drapery—he points with his tiny feminine hand—becomes ornamental.

Ornamental might be a description of the man himself. No, Muhlbach thinks, 'affected' would be better. How contemptuous of us he is.

Next is a fantastic bronze or brass receptacle in the form of an ogre with clumsy paws and a curly tail. The beast is devouring a human who doesn't seem to mind. From ears to tail this strange object is etched with intricate geometrical patterns.

Your liquid container of the *yu* type. Shang, naturally, which will place it ten to fifteen centuries before Christ. The oldest work on display. The shape, dimensions and adornment of these vessels varied according to usage. They were classified and named by scholars of the Sung period, frequently on the basis of a dedicatory inscription. Thus you have your *ku,* shaped like a slender wine glass widening at the top, your *chueh,* which is a tripod bowl with a beak-like handle, and so forth.

He leads the group toward a smiling limestone personage whose right hand is raised in a pontifical blessing—an example of the angular style which dominated the Wei period during the fourth century. Guests are allowed half a minute to look at it.

He directs them to another bizarre creation. A chimera from that same period. The sacred and the profane embodied.

Eula shudders. She recoils from the porcelain beast with a dramatic show of disgust.

Ascher walks quickly into the next room, where he stops. He folds his arms. Nothing is in this room except two gigantic temple guards in baggy pantaloons whose topknots almost brush the ceiling. Beyond doubt they were meant to intimidate whoever looked at them—from the monstrous feet to the eyes bulging with insane rage.

What you see, he remarks in his querulous tenor voice, may be the finest matched pair in the United States. The absolute soul of my collection.

What we are hearing, Muhlbach says to himself, is a consummate snob. And having gazed at the wooden giants for a few seconds he concludes that he would rather have the T'ang lady. From a sculptural point of view these are quite possibly superb. Ascher may be justified in calling them the finest in the United States. They are unique and terrifying, provided one is willing to be terrified by a preposterous overstatement. But finally what matters is whether or not you identify with the spirit of a work.

Ascher snaps off the floodlight and walks past another electric eye into a third room.

He pauses beside a black pedestal. This will display his newest acquisition—a bronze altar of the Nara period—which is en route from Japan. He describes it. Three figures resting on lotus flowers. He feels privileged to have obtained the altar because the Honolulu Academy of Arts was about to buy it.

Now this would be your Nara, he continues, pointing at a grimacing warrior who is so infuriated by the enemy that his carved hair seems to be afire. Prissy and I both were overwhelmed by this big blustery Meikira when we encountered him in Kyoto.

Now here—he points to an eight-armed metal deity holding a scepter—you have your Kannon. In terms of balance and expressiveness the work is adequate, but as you can see twelve centuries have exacted their toll.

He waits a few moments, answers questions, walks briskly toward the next pedestal.

Sages, guardians, more Bodhisattvas. A headless marble torso. Three gilded masks judiciously arranged on the wall. He identifies each work by its period, offers a comment or so, and urges his flock forward like an impatient shepherd.

Well, thinks Muhlbach, I've had enough. As far as I'm concerned these statues look as much alike as so many fish. Either they're angry or they're self-satisfied, and although I respect the craftsmanship it seems to me that everything has been stylized. Tradition, I suppose. More or less the same as medieval Christian art—those rigid heraldic madonnas and kings and crucifixions. Not to my taste. This sculpture has dignity, which I do like. But so much repetitious melodramatic fury and such determined serenity—no, I can't relate to it. Except for one or two things his collection is a staggering bore.

A glance at Eula confirms his guess that she, too, has had enough. In fact she looks a little apprehensive. One can produce only so many exclamations of rapture, fright, astonishment or whatever else seems appropriate. Yet from now on she will maintain that this tour of Dr. Ascher's gallery was one of the most thrilling experiences of her life.

And Eula isn't alone. The other guests, to judge by their attitudes, are every bit as intimidated. How strange.

The final room belongs to Prissy. On a fragile cherrywood table stands a yellow vase with a bouquet of fresh flowers. Nearby is a filing cabinet, a couple of chairs and a collapsible wooden rack supporting a large peppermint-stripe portfolio. Paintings have been hung indiscriminately—delicate evocations of wild geese, pines, waterfalls, goldfish. Muhlbach stares at them with a feeling of surprise. How difficult to predict someone's taste. Prissy is so chic, so desperately avant. But instead of the latest thing, whatever the latest thing might be, she prefers traditional art.

Ascher, discussing the paintings, subtly manages to indicate that they are not worth the attention of a serious collector:

Momoyama period. Hasegawa Tohaku, an unusual artist who excelled in the characteristically Chinese medium of ink monochrome.

Not a word of criticism, nevertheless it's clear that he bought these paintings only because his wife wanted them. Furthermore, he wants the visitors to realize it. What insufferable conceit.

Ascher, almost as if he divined the thought, releases the group and turns his intelligent scornful gaze on Muhlbach.

What about you, sir? You've said very little.

I've said nothing whatever, Muhlbach thinks. What could I say? The T'ang lady was appealing, but that's about all. Should I say the rest of the collection puts me to sleep?

Eula informs me that you, too, are a collector.

Eula would call a wigwam a skyscraper. I have one small pre-Columbian piece.

Pre-Columbian, Ascher remarks. Pre-Columbian. Then you must be acquainted with the screenwriter Claude Varda.

No.

I don't recall how many films Claude has done— *Johnny Payola. Guns to Laredo, Horns for the Devil, Down Payment*—which is neither here nor there. Claude spent a year in Atlanta for contempt of Congress during the tenure of our de facto President Joseph McCarthy. Upon his release he moved to Mexico for a spell of recuperation where he met, among others, Diego Rivera. As you no doubt know,

Rivera was a devout collector of pre-Columbiana and I believe it may have been Rivera who got Claude started. Give him a ring, if you care to. Feel free to use my name.

Thank you, I might.

I have offered you an introduction to a sophisticated collector, which I almost never do, and your response is 'Thank you, I might.' Ascher's pinched face trembles with exasperation. His voice has caused several of the guests to turn around.

Good Lord, Muhlbach thinks, what did he expect? I suppose I should have kissed his feet. He's out of his mind. I've never seen such arrogance. Well, Dr. Ascher, if I could permit myself to be as rude to you as you have been to me I would say that I find your half-ton Buddhas and your infuriated wooden giants a colossal waste of time. You're as myopic as Holmgren with his God damned Tlingit baskets. And besides, you can't even remember my name.

Ascher presumably feels that further discussion would be useless. Without so much as a nod he returns to the group.

Xylography, Muhlbach can hear him say, is the proper term for the art of woodblock, which was invented three centuries ago by Moronobu. Moronobu's technique, however commendable, was subsequently much improved upon by the celebrated Harunobu. Pictures of the passing world—*ukiyo-e*— they are called, because they delineate everyday customs, events and persons. It would take too long to explain the social and economic policies of Shogun Tokugawa Ieyasu which gave rise to this particular artistic manifestation, so I shall oversimplify and merely tell you that the Japanese woodblock emerged in response to a new and widespread public appreciation of art.

He opens the portfolio and begins turning the

prints rather quickly, perhaps to make up for the minutes wasted talking to a pre-Columbian collector.

Your Shigemasa—an artist of limited stature. Nonetheless a meticulous craftsman sensitive to contemporary fashion. Notice the maidservant's kimono. Imported material such as calico and velvet became popular in Japan during the late seventies.

Next, your Eisho. Chokosai Eisho. Usually considered the most talented of the great Eishi's pupils. What we have in this instance is a first impression with extensive retouching. I would call the condition of this print average or below average because of certain defects in the paper, the horizontal crease, moderate wormage and slight marginal staining. Eisho. A superior workman.

He pauses to let his guests examine the Eisho.

Astonishing, Muhlbach thinks. The man must be someplace else. He isn't here. Only a body and a recorded voice.

So, if the tour of Dr. Ascher's private museum has not been as delightful as Eula predicted, at least it could be considered instructive. I can't pretend that I like him, Muhlbach reflects. I wonder if anybody does. Still, I did learn a thing or two and that's what counts.

The thought of telephoning Varda is mildly unpleasant and he attempts to forget it, but several days later he finds himself frowning at the directory.

I'll just take a look, he tells himself. The fellow won't be listed and I certainly don't intend to call Ascher, so that'll be that. I'll just make sure he's not in the book.

There are very few Vardas in the entire metropolitan area. However, one of them is Claude.

Reluctantly, with the conviction that his life is now being directed by some nameless and perhaps malignant goddess, he dials the number. It is nine o'clock on a Saturday night. Varda will not be home.

As the telephone goes on ringing Muhlbach's troubled frown begins to lift. One or two more rings should be enough.

Yeh?

Mr. Varda?

Yeh.

My name is Muhlbach. Dr. David Ascher suggested I call.

Ascher? Oh yeh. So what's on your mind?

Varda is direct, if nothing else. Evidently he has no use for bourgeois preliminaries. All right, get to the point before he hangs up.

Pre-Columbian art.

A moment of silence during which Muhlbach hears laughter in the background. Then Varda replies in a less challenging voice:

Couple of God damn noisy friends. What did you say your name was?

And it's as simple as that. Once you discover a man's passion the rest is easy. Suspicion fades, barriers drop. Barbershop quartets, harness racing, golf, square dancing, Dusenbergs, the best way to cook liver and onions—all that's necessary is to pluck the needle from the haystack.

Look, Muhlbach, jump in a cab.

You're inviting me over? Now?

Jesus Christ! You want to talk pre-Columbian on the phone?

I'm practically on my way. I understand you have quite a collection.

Yeh. Top floor. Push the button three times.

What an extraordinary invitation, Muhlbach reflects. What am I getting into?

By ten o'clock he is in Varda's East River penthouse with a drink on his knee and the screenwriter's name has begun to sound familiar. Some of his movies may have reappeared on television. At any rate, there's no doubt about his success. He has a large choice apartment in the seventies and what at first looked like a bowling trophy on the coffee table has turned out to be a Hollywood Oscar.

His noisy friends are a lanky old director named Jack Henry with ravaged features and an aluminum patch over one eye who is dressed in filthy jodphurs, and Henry's plump nubile protégée who can't be more than seventeen—Cheryl somebody—outfitted in scuffed cowboy boots and faded denims with daisies embroidered on the seat.

Varda, too, is stylishly dressed. His ensemble consists of an airline mechanic's coveralls zipped to the neck and frayed sneakers but no socks. He has a smoker's flabby face with a thick yellowish mustache, waxed and pointed, curling skyward as though hinting that once upon a time he was a daredevil pilot. He attends to the mustache, obviously. Otherwise he needs a shave.

Waving toward his collection he growls, I got a hunger for this crap. It's like nothing else, Muhlbach.

He picks up a masked Colima dancer wearing a fantastic helmet. The mask and helmet can be removed.

Got this bugger for a few pesos. Used to go out to the site and watch them dig. Whenever they turned up a good piece I'd buy it. Hell, twenty years ago you could name your price. They were digging up so much Colima they didn't know what to do with it. Even in those days you had to watch out because they'd fake important pieces, but I knew this baby was good. The guy who brought it to me swore he'd found it himself, which is enough to make anybody suspicious, but it felt right. Just the same I took it to one of those museum creeps to have it checked. I said is this thing good? The son of a bitch was afraid to say yes or no, but I kept after him. Finally he said to me—this is what he said: 'In my opinion national treasures should be returned to the country of origin.' You know what I told him? I told him to go screw himself.

Varda reaches into an ashtray for the cold stump of a cigar and begins chewing it.

He picks up an Olmec paint pot. Hemispherical, cream-colored, just the right size to hold in the palm of your hand. He dips an index finger behind the rim and then wipes his wrist, leaving a reddish brown stain.

Powdered hematite, Muhlbach.

He picks up a Casas Grandes anthropomorphic bowl from the thirteenth century with a classic Greek profile, the arms and legs modeled in bas relief. Black, ivory and red, decorated with precise triangles, circles, loops and labyrinths. The bowl is in perfect condition, not so much as a pressure crack. The eyes of the effigy are almost shut. The nostrils and the gently smiling lips are clogged by the residue of the corpse with which it was buried.

Look at this fat bastard, Varda growls around the wet cigar. Nothing in Mexico City to touch it. Might be the God damnedest Casas Grandes in existence. What do you think, Muhlbach? You seen a better one?

The questions, of course, are rhetorical.

He picks up one bowl after another. His eyes glow and his lips pucker with excitement. The masked dancer may be more valuable, sculpturally more difficult, artistically more important, but it's plain that he loves bowls the way Ascher loves marble Buddhas or Holmgren loves wicker baskets.

He displays a thin-walled orange bowl from Guatemala, from the ruins of Tikal, similar in shape to the Olmec paint pot but much larger, flat on the bottom, turned with scrupulous grace, as symmetrical as if its maker had known of the potter's wheel. The surface is faintly nicked and striated, the muted orange color clouded here and there with microscopic growths. Highly burnished, it looks as hard as porcelain.

Tap the son of a bitch with your fingernail, Varda insists. Break it and I'll shoot you.

Muhlbach obeys cautiously, remembering how Quimby tapped the Jaina figurine with a pencil. The bowl clinks like a metal goblet.

What do you think? Seen anything better?

Oh wow! says Cheryl, lying on a rug at the director's feet. She lifts her head to stare at the bowl with a dreamy smile and dilated eyes.

Jack Henry leans down, offering her the sweet brown cigarette.

It occurs to Muhlbach that a scene very much like this might have taken place centuries ago in one of the Tikal apartments. The sickening smoke would be the same and Mayan words of praise might not have been too different.

Wow! That one blows my mind.

Varda, munching the cigar, replies thoughtfully: Yeh kid, you and me both. Look here, Muhlbach. Maybe the best frigging calligraphy on earth.

He points to the glyphs around the rim—a black procession of incomprehensible symbols, ominous faces neither animal nor human, at once realistic and abstract, each as sharply linear as the pattern on a Chou or Shang vase. A less accomplished craftsman would have embellished the space with extravagant painting—birds, snakes, deities, ball players, sacrificial victims, priests with scrolls issuing from their mouths. But this potter was so sophisticated, so confident, that he could refrain from demonstrating his skill.

Varda explains that only a few glyphs can be deciphered, thanks to the first Bishop of Yucatán, Diego de Landa, a typical servant of the Lord who scoured the peninsula for Indian books and burned as many as he could find. These books, the Bishop

knew beyond doubt, were filled with nothing but
superstition and lies of the devil. He found plenty
of them, by his own account, and reduced them to
ashes. Three escaped the holocaust. Three! says
Varda emphatically. Can you imagine the son of
a bitch?

The best of these manuscripts is now in Dresden.
It concerns the periods of rotation of the planet
Venus and is assumed to be a faithful replica of a
still earlier manuscript. Another, concerned with a
series of prophecies based on the twenty-year *katun*
cycle and the twenty-times-twenty *baktun*, is in the
Bibliothèque Nationale in Paris. Poorly preserved,
it was rediscovered in 1887 under a pile of trash
with a wrapper on which had been written in six-
teenth-century script the name 'Perez.' The last and
most extensive of these three books is now in Ma-
drid. It consists of ritual prescriptions and, like the
Dresden codex, is thought to be a copy of an older
manuscript—but copied quickly and rudely, maybe
by a priest who needed it for personal use.

Far out, says Cheryl in the strangled voice that
Muhlbach has learned to identify. She speaks without letting go of the smoke in her lungs and lolls on
the rug like a turnip—stupefied, witless, happy. For
a girl that age she looks suspiciously thick around
the waist. He glances at Jack Henry. The haggard
old roué is preparing another cigarette.

Varda has returned to the subject of bowls. The
very best bowls are found in an area inhabited by
the Mayans, from the Gulf of Campeche as far south
as Guatemala and British Honduras. Bowls from
the Pacific slope, from the states of Nayarit and
Colima and Guerrero, from the central Mexican
plateau and the Mixtec sites of Oaxaca—yes, some
good stuff has turned up there, but the great bowls,
the classics—a type they call 'thin orange' manufactured around Puebla, exported to cities as far

apart as Teotihuacán and Kaminalijuyú—cylindrical polychrome—marine motifs—carved before firing—Chama—Maya heartland . . .

Muhlbach, feeling rather drunk, slumped in a chair beside the fireplace, listens solemnly. This world is so new, this ancient world. And why does it amaze me? he wonders. Because these New World relics do astound me. Because they're unfamiliar? Because we were taught as children to appreciate almost nothing except Greco-Roman art?

He considers the Tikal bowl, a gleaming orange hemisphere adorned with mysterious glyphs painted a thousand years ago, and Varda's obsession seems perfectly reasonable.

I'm warning you, Muhlbach, you can get hooked on this stuff. Look there.

He points to a cracked vessel which must have been exceptionally beautiful when it was new. Now the red and yellow panels are encrusted with a cement-like substance.

Just look at the old hag. You ever see anything in worse shape? But I love her. I couldn't give her up.

Far out! Cheryl cries in that congested voice.

What would her passion be?

Life. To get the most from every minute. She sucks up another draft of smoke, her schoolgirl face momentarily tense and expectant.

The atmosphere is so sweet that Muhlbach wonders if his suit will have to be cleaned. It might be smart to wear something else to the office on Monday.

As for Jack Henry? Well, his passion is plain enough.

Varda shows off a Mixtec tripod vase and then a Totonac gooseneck from Cerro de las Mesas. Then a small blue-black vase shining like a gun barrel, its handle in the form of a coyote's head, pale blue paint around the rim.

Plumbate ware from Tula. Look.

He takes down from the shelf an alabaster urn with a tattooed human face.

Look here, Muhlbach.

A bright orange terra cotta shell with a grinning dwarf inside.

Look.

Yes, Muhlbach thinks as he holds the incredible shell in both hands, if I were rich and could afford a passion this is how I'd ruin myself.

On top of the bookcase stands a tiny Tlatilco dancer.

Diego gave me that. Christ, I love it! Do you like it?

But without waiting for an answer he goes on:

You been to Mexico? I spent a couple years there after they let me out of the can. I guess you heard about it. Everybody else has. I couldn't get work here because of that McCarthy bastard so I was doing scripts under a pseudonym in Mexico. The place was crotch-deep in Communists, which is how I met Diego. Great guy. I loved the porky little son of a bitch.

Half an hour later the subject is Chichimec pottery.

By two o'clock Jack Henry and Cheryl have retired to a bedroom, but as the night wears away Varda becomes more and more loquacious. He walks back and forth patting his belly, gesticulating, describing marvelous pre-Columbian pieces he has seen in other collections. Schwartz. Bliss. Spratling. Kaiser. La Boyteaux.

At three o'clock Muhlbach gets up. It's time to leave.

Varda looks surprised, then disappointed. He thrusts his hands into the pockets of his coveralls.

Okay, if you got to. Hell, glad you dropped by. Give me a ring anytime. Like to see that Jaina.

You're off to a good start. Yeh, bring along that Jaina.

I will. I'd appreciate your opinion.

Sounds like a winner.

At the price I could hardly lose.

Varda takes the cigar out of his mouth in order to be emphatic. Listen, Muhlbach. Forget money. If you try to save a few bucks you end up with crap. Travel first class.

I'll keep that in mind.

Buenas noches.

Goodnight.

Buenas noches indeed. What a night. The Colima masked dancer, the Olmec paint pot containing traces of a prehistoric artist's pigment, Rivera's gift, Tula plumbate ware, a bowl from Tikal, that Mixtec tripod, the elegant gooseneck from Cerro de las Mesas—yes, and the shell with the dwarf inside— Varda is traveling first class, no question about it. But how does one ride up front if one doesn't have the money? The answer is simple. One doesn't.

So for now, and perhaps for some time to come, Muhlbach thinks, I'll be traveling tourist. In other words, I might as well see what Mr. Piglett has to offer. A truckload of junk, no doubt. However, we'll see what we'll see. The twentieth, Holmgren said. All right, I'll go. I wonder if I should invite Eula. She'd love it. No. No, she might feel inspired to create a costume for the occasion and I just couldn't walk into that motel with Eula impersonating a squaw. I'd better go alone.

ON February eighteenth an ad appears in the classified section: WESTERN AMERICANA! Attention collectors! Tremendous inventory! Hundreds of items. Navajo rugs. Jewelry. Buffalo coat. Sand paintings. Kachinas. Trade beads. Old guns. Coral necklaces. Arrowheads. San Ildefonso pottery. Fetishes. Swords. Authentic tomahawks. Rare Yurok baskets. Belt buckles. Genuine fossils. Argillite. Ivory carvings. Religious relics. Spurs. Rattles. Purses. Wells Fargo strongbox. Conchos. Early Sioux moccasins. Much more. Alaskan Eskimo. Northwest Coast. Pre-Columbian. Moundbuilder. Plains. California. Chance of a Lifetime! Seagrave's Hi-Way House, Queens. Feb. 20 at 7:30. Preview at 6. Auctioneer: J. W. Piglett.

Shortly after seven o'clock on that date as he emerges from the revolving door Muhlbach hears a soft familiar voice:

Hello.

Holmgren!

He looks the same—that cheap brown suit and the same shirt blooming with poisonous brilliance. No doubt it finds a motel climate congenial. Holmgren's face, though, does look a little different. Why? Devilish forked beard, apprehensive eyes distorted by those binoculars—no change there. Ah! The California tan is gone, washed away like stage makeup. He's as gray as a night watchman. Maybe he's sick.

His mournful smile is so tentative. Holmgren, Holmgren. Is life so hard? Have you met nothing but brickbats and insults?

How's Quetzalcóatl?

The Mayan, of course. Holmgren's attempt at levity.

Quetzalcóatl is fine. Though I suspect he disapproves of our New York weather.

Don't we all. Hey, can I buy you a drink?

Holmgren needs a bath. And his fingernails have yet to be cleaned. I'd rather inspect the merchandise, Muhlbach thinks. But then he feels ashamed of himself for hesitating.

No, this should be my treat. If I remember correctly you bought us a round somewhere above Oklahoma.

Holmgren blinks and shyly agrees.

Inside the cocktail lounge he seems a bit less soiled, perhaps because he's less visible. The sport shirt meshes with the floral wallpaper.

After drinks have been ordered Muhlbach decides it would be polite to mention baskets. Ask a few questions about baskets before directing the conversation toward what really matters.

Holmgren replies that some of the boxes have not been unpacked yet, but he saw a stack of Papago coils and a Third Mesa Hopi.

Nervously twisting a button of his suit he goes on: I could use a Third Mesa. A friend of mine's got sixteen of them. And I sure would like a good Wasco sally-bag. Talk about scarce. Listen, pal, Wes told me in California they were going out of sight. Same with Chehalis.

If Piglett tells you that a certain basket is scarce do you take his word for it?

Wes won't bull the regulars. He can't afford to.

I gather you've done some business at these auctions. Do you feel you've gotten your money's worth?

Holmgren nods and seems about to elaborate. Muhlbach hurriedly changes the subject.

Did Piglett bring any pre-Columbian?

Holmgren plucks at his beard. He doesn't notice much except baskets. But now he remembers. Yes, there were a few pots that looked pretty old. Not tourist stuff.

Mayan? Zapotec? Casas Grandes?

Pots, pots. All pots look alike.

What about effigies?

Holmgren scratches his scalp and then inspects his fingernail. He can't be sure if there were any effigies because they aren't his thing. But there was a big green stone mask.

What culture?

Maybe Aztec. Maybe Toltec. Maybe something else.

What shape? Triangular? Trapezoidal?

More like this.

He forms an oval with his fingertips not quite touching.

What about the expression? Could you describe that? For instance, would you call it 'snarling'? Did it remind you of a jaguar?

Holmgren wants a moment to think about this. Finally he answers that it did look like a jaguar.

Or a fat crying baby?

I guess so. Sure, you could describe it like that.

Good God, Muhlbach thinks, it's an Olmec. They're auctioning an Olmec.

Wow! Holmgren murmurs. If you could see yourself. My wife gives me the business every time I go to an auction. Baskets, she says. Howard, if you come home with one more basket I'll divorce you. If she could see you—oh wow!

Muhlbach looks at him in astonishment. An Olmec jade is going up for auction and he compares it to a wicker basket. Incredible. But there's something else to consider. If Holmgren doesn't realize the value of an Olmec jade it's just possible that nobody else will.

What sort of a crowd should we expect?

Hard to say.

What about dealers? Do you expect any dealers?

Maybe.

Muhlbach begins to feel frustrated. Now look here, these auctions may be old hat for you but I'm anxious to see that mask and whatever else Piglett brought along.

Holmgren agreeably empties his drink, drops a handful of peanuts into his coat pocket and makes his way through the gloomy cocktail lounge with supreme confidence. Muhlbach stumbles after him, wondering if he sees better in the dark.

The auction will not be held in Piglett's suite but in the Colonial Room, which has been outfitted for the occasion with a speaker's platform, a microphone, a phalanx of banquet tables and about two hundred folding chairs. Boxes of artifacts are still being unpacked but a good many prospective bidders already are examining the merchandise, which is strewn across the tables like the stock of a bankrupt country store. Each item wears a numbered tag.

Piglett is easy to identify. He's a long way from southern California in a western shirt with red glass buttons, black whipcord pants with slash pockets, two-tone boots and a Wyatt Earp mustache. A thick silver buckle supports his paunch, glinting in the light as he tramps around behind the tables in search of something, followed by three boys wearing tight new Levi's who are unmistakably his sons—all three with shoulder-length Buffalo Bill curls and their father's little yellow-brown eyes. The oldest boy wears a tall Mexican sombrero and the second one carries a pair of leather gloves protruding from his hip pocket. The youngest hasn't yet come up with a trademark but before much longer he will adopt a buckskin vest or figured boots or possibly a gold watch chain. After all, one must announce one's presence to the world, even though the world may not care.

Muhlbach looks again at Piglett. Except for being overweight he could be called handsome in an ugly western way, or at least he used to be handsome. Now he's obviously spending too much time at supper. Just above his belt one glass button has popped off, revealing the white elastic waistband of his shorts and a slice of hairy belly. He stomps across the platform and pauses to survey the crowd—hands on his hips, head thrust forward in that peculiar round-shouldered challenging stance of westerners, topaz eyes gleaming as if he was about to draw and shoot.

Come on, pal, says Holmgren, I'll introduce you.

They catch up with Piglett at the cash box where he is talking to a strawberry blonde in an expensive rodeo suit—presumably his wife. She wears a small diamond engagement ring with a matched wedding band. Her hair has been teased into a pneumatic beehive, sprayed until it resembles pink cotton candy. She would be in her thirties, a thinly muscular woman who could be considered attractive if it weren't for the preposterous construction on top of her head. Not beautiful, perhaps. Her jaw is masculine. But she would be less brittle, less like the queen of a roller derby, without that coiffure.

Glad you made it, says Piglett when Muhlbach is introduced. Meet Dixie.

Dixie has the voice and the grip of a Texas rancher.

Put your name on the mailing list, Piglett continues. Holmgren here can tell you how everything works.

And with a hearty slap on the back he's off again

to scout the territory—bushy sideburns, handlebar mustache, bow-legged and gross, trailed by three juvenile bandits.

Muhlbach discovers that he is doing just what Piglett suggested. After he has put down his name and address Dixie gives him a bidding card and a mimeographed catalogue.

Halfway down the second table between a cellophane bag of turquoise nuggets and a framed collection of arrowheads is the mask. The number on the tag is 129. He looks it up in the catalogue.

Huge Mexican jadeite mask. Very rare.

The stone feels hard, not like soapstone or the dyed green Mexican onyx bookends for sale in department stores. Stylistically it looks Olmec.

He stares at the mask, turns it over to examine the smooth concavity of the back, turns it face up to study the bloated features. If indeed it is an Olmec piece and not an imitation it must be invaluable.

He takes out his keys. The office key is more or less pointed, so he grasps it firmly and attempts to make a slight scratch on the bottom of the mask. There is no sensation of metal biting into stone. He tries again, dragging the key heavily across the surface, but the stone can't be marked. He takes out his handkerchief, wets it on his tongue and rubs the stone. Nothing comes off, so it seems unlikely that a dye has been used.

He looks closely at the eye sockets, at the holes drilled in the ear lobes and at both corners of the snarling mouth.

I ought to have a lens, he thinks. One of those gadgets Quimby carries around. In any case, what have we got here? Is this a fake or is it a couple of thousand years old?

After replacing the mask on the table he steps back and squints.

It looks right. It may be good. I think it is. It's real, I think. It looks so much like that color photograph in Dockstader.

He picks it up again, shuts his eyes and tries to sense through his fingertips whether it was laboriously carved by some prehistoric Indian using primitive tools or whether it was manufactured with the help of a power drill in a Mexico City machine shop. And as he fondles the mask he becomes persuaded.

Yes, he says to himself. Yes. I don't quite know how I know, but I know. This is no fake.

Then it occurs to him that in Taos when he first saw the Mayan he was not concerned about authenticity. What mattered was the object itself. He had liked the Mayan. Just looking at it was a pleasure. That was why he had bought it. Now, inexplicably, these values have been transposed and the important consideration is whether or not the mask is a genuine Olmec. Aesthetic appeal doesn't matter so much.

The implications of this are not exactly comforting.

A moment after he lets go of the mask, two leather-fringed hippies stop by, reeking of Bombay perfume, their eyes dilated.

Hey dig, one of them mumbles with a stupefied smile.

Groovy, man.

What a trip.

Far out.

I mean, heavy.

Too much.

This stimulating exchange of ideas promises to continue, so Muhlbach draws a circle around No. 129 and moves along.

A brace of rusty dueling pistols in a faded velvet box, a concho belt, garish ceramic trade beads, a gilded frame of arrowheads, dirty moccasins, a medicine pouch decorated with porcupine quills, an old Bowie knife with a nicked blade, a clay pipe, bannerstones, shells clumsily inlaid with abalone—the table is littered with such rubbish. Why would anybody want it? Yet people are examining this junk and making notes.

Holmgren is gravely feeling a threadbare blanket. Has he decided to get into something other than baskets? No. No, but this happens to be an early Germantown. Not many of these around. Probably 1885 or 1890. Should bring about fifty dollars.

Muhlbach picks up an odd little brownstone animal carrying a packet of shells, beads and feathers on its back. What would this be?

A Zuñi fetish. A mole, hunter-god of the nether regions. The packet increases its power. Most fetishes are bears or mountain lions, sometimes a wolf or an eagle or a coyote. A mole is rare. Furthermore, this isn't a commercial fetish. This has been used in ceremonies. Look at the age on the feathers. Look at the condition of the leather thong.

How much is it worth?

Holmgren inspects the stone. Not much turquoise, mostly matrix. But genuine fetishes are scarce. Twenty dollars. Maybe more if some dealer wants it.

What about baskets? Anything unusual?

Yes. Holmgren has found a half-twist overlay. Yurok. First quality. He'd love to get it. But that bitch is here, he says, making no effort to conceal his hatred. He points to a middle-aged woman in a Persian lamb coat and horn-rimmed glasses.

She doesn't know what's good. She waits to see what I want and then ups it a buck. Last time she took a beautiful Salish right out of my hands. But I fixed her. I bid her up to thirty on a new Bella Coola with a tear in the rim. Worth ten bucks at most—at most! Holmgren cackles savagely and strokes his beard.

He points to another table. Wes brought along some Maya stuff.

But the Mayan offering turns out to be a disappointment. A few reconstructed bowls, probably authentic, so crudely glued together and of so little artistic interest in the first place that they are hardly worth evaluating. A string of unremarkable beads. A scrap of bone on which somebody—perhaps Piglett or one of his bandit sons—has scratched the outline of a snake. A fragment of mottled gray granite, identified in the catalogue as a ceremonial ax. And four Jaina figurines—fakes. They don't deserve to be called fakes. Copies would be more appropriate. Each one is different, yet they're all alike, obviously manufactured. The surface has been aged with dirt and ink and paint and acid. The famous Mayan blue has been more or less imitated with dimestore watercolors. Fine sandpaper probably was used to blunt the nose and lips, and what might be shoe polish has been smeared over random areas in an attempt to duplicate the stain left by a disintegrating corpse. No, it would be a compliment to call them fakes. Imitations they are, and any amateur should know they were fresh from the factory. Yet in terms of sculptural form they aren't bad, which suggests that the factory might be using original Mayan molds.

Muhlbach looks them up in the catalogue. Nos. 212–215. Mexican idols. No description. Well, at least Piglett isn't trying to palm them off as authentic.

On the same table is something quite a lot more important—a married couple made of clay, seated tandem fashion, the male in front and his wife grasping his waist as though they were riding a motorcycle. Distinctive crisscross headbands and elongated features identify them as being from Jalisco.

No. 238. Joined couple. Man holding rattle. 16″

tall. Black and red painted decoration. 3rd–5th century. Jalisco. Ameca Gray type. Extremely rare.

The piece shows a certain amount of erosion, the usual nicks and scratches and one hairline crack. Otherwise it appears to be in excellent shape. The modeling is good, both faces treated with sensitivity. The balance is good. The pose is formal to the point of being hieratic, yet the two figures are welded by a mysterious inner tension. They seem to be traveling the stream of life together, the man staring blindly ahead, his wife staring blindly to one side. And that they do represent a man with his wife instead of two frivolous companions can hardly be doubted.

Muhlbach carefully turns the piece around.

On the opposite side the red paint has been destroyed below a well defined level, suggesting that it had sunk this far into the earth when the tomb was opened. The wife's left ear lobe has been broken off, evidently quite a while ago. And there's another crack, more serious, starting at the man's foot and extending through his thigh. Nevertheless, the piece is relatively undamaged.

Muhlbach continues to stare at it. Yes. Yes, I'd like to have this, he thinks. It's stronger than those I've seen in the books. I wonder what it'll go for. Holmgren might be able to give me an estimate, but in any event we'll just have to wait and see. First I've got to try for the Olmec. The Olmec comes first.

He glances again at the tag: No. 238. He circles it on the list and is about to resume browsing when suddenly he feels a pair of yellowish eyes. Not far away stands Piglett.

See any goodies?

I haven't finished looking.

Somebody interrupts to ask Piglett a question. Muhlbach uses the moment to drift away.

Corroded hotel keys, silver dollars, saddle blankets, an old horsehair lariat, the skin of an ermine, trays of turquoise and coral jewelry, prehistoric axes, more arrowheads, painted tin icons, cheap clay owls, a bear claw necklace, mortars and pestles, a beaver hat—it's really not far from this to a Lewis Carroll world of ships, shoes, cabbages and sealing wax.

A few minutes later Piglett taps the microphone and blows into it. One, two, three. Testing. Testing.

The crowd begins to leave the tables.

Muhlbach decides on another quick look at his two discoveries, but an old man with a tangled beard and trembling fingers is examining the Jalisco. All at once the old man sticks out his tongue and licks the statue. Apparently he's trying to detect something, but what? Can he tell from the taste of the paint if those are modern chemicals? Well, right now there isn't time to discuss the matter.

The Olmec has been moved across the table and is almost hidden by the corner of a folded blanket. Muhlbach picks it up, scrapes at a discolored spot beside the mouth, peers at the burnished surface for any indication of metal tools, compares it in his mind with the illustrations of famous Olmec masks, and becomes more than ever persuaded. Just how long ago this menacing jaguar-child was carved is impossible to say, but the emphasis on geometric design would suggest a middle pre-classic date, more or less contemporary with the Periclean age of Greece. Maybe earlier, he reflects. If this came from La Venta it might be earlier. Extraordinary. What I'm holding in my hands might have been buried for a thousand years when Marcus Aurelius was born.

After fingering the mask and weighing it, deliberating until the last minute, he replaces it on the table and looks around for Holmgren.

Holmgren has taken a seat in the back row where he is polishing his glasses. His feeble blinking eyes, unprotected, seem to bulge with terror. However he's not terrified, just annoyed by the lady in the Persian lamb coat.

That bitch, he remarks, and stops to hook the glasses over his ears. Listen, Muhlbach, I got a favor to ask because if she finds out I'm bidding on the Yurok she'll raise me.

What he has in mind is plain enough. No, I don't like this, Muhlbach thinks. Not at all. I don't want to bid for him. I doubt if he's a crook, but I'm not sure. And that woman—I'd better watch out.

Then he begins to feel guilty. Holmgren couldn't be a swindler, he's too naive. And that woman with her awful painted mouth and galoshes half unzipped —she must be exactly what she appears to be. Piglett is not to be trusted, and there may very well be collaborators in the audience, but Holmgren is as genuine as he is unfortunate.

How much are you willing to pay?

No more than sixty. What about the mask? You going for it?

Yes. how much will it bring?

If it's real, plenty.

You sound suspicious.

Maybe it's okay. How should I know? Pre-Columbian's not my bag.

Piglett flicks the microphone a few times with his finger in order to get attention and then makes a little introductory speech. He is glad to see such a good crowd. He points out that American Indian and frontier relics are becoming scarce and this may be one of the last chances to pick up authentic examples at a bargain price.

You dealers in the audience, he continues. You know what I'm talking about. You've seen prices double every year these last few years. Those of you who go to the West Coast on buying trips remember the items you could pick up a year or two ago for practically nothing. Now they'd cost a fortune—if we could get them. And you collectors—those of you who have been to these auctions before—you know what's happening to prices. Three years ago in San Francisco I got twenty dollars for a Mandan vest that should have been in a museum. Today a vest like that—if I could find another one—would bring a hundred dollars. Maybe more. Maybe two hundred—I don't know. So don't be afraid to bid on things you want. If it sounds like too much money just think what it'll cost next year. And if you can't afford it right now we can hold it for you with a small down payment. We accept personal checks with proper identification and if you've got a special problem about paying for an item—why, go ahead and bid on it and talk it over with us after the show. We'll work out some kind of arrangement. There are a lot of items on these tables you won't ever have the opportunity to buy again, so don't be bashful. For a few dollars you may pick up a Dakota war club that was used at the Little Big Horn. I don't know half of what we got here—we might even have Custer's scalp.

He signals to his oldest boy. Okay, Jeff, let's get started.

Jeff, who has been sitting on the edge of the platform moodily chewing a toothpick, hops off and shuffles across to the first table. He holds up a rusty branding iron.

Number one on your list. Double F iron from the old Frazier ranch. Laramie, Wyoming. I've been on that ranch myself many a time. This iron was used maybe as early as 1860. Who'll give a thousand dollars?

Piglett waits for the laughter to subside.

You got to think big once in a while, folks. Who'll give a dollar?

Several cards go up.

Now everybody wants it! That's always the way. Who'll give two? Two here in front. Now three? Three, thank you. Four? Everybody wants it. Five? Six? Who'll give six? And now seven?

The branding iron goes for eight dollars.

Next is a painted wooden doll with a grotesque blue face and feathers on its arms.

Who'll give five hundred for this Hopi eagle kachina? The Hopis have more kachinas than you can count and a lot of people ask why they need so many, but the Hopis can't figure out why we need thirty thousand saints. This one's not an old one, but you're never going to see a better one. Who'll give four hundred dollars? How about one hundred? Fifty? Twenty? Sure! Everybody wants it. Now twenty-five. Now thirty.

The kachina brings forty. Muhlbach is amazed. And if a wooden doll brings forty dollars it looks bad for the Olmec.

But who knows how much things are worth? A large frame of arrowheads brings nine dollars. A mountain lion fetish with coral eyes brings thirty. One cellophane packet of Indian head pennies sells for five dollars while another, apparently identical, sells for eight. A handsome bright red blanket goes for twenty, then a moth-eaten shabby Arapaho chief's blanket sells for sixty-five.

While the chief's blanket is being folded by Piglett's two younger sons Holmgren nods wisely.

See the guy who got the Arapaho? He's a dealer. He'll put that blanket in the window and ask two hundred.

Muhlbach looks at the dealer, who is writing something in a little notebook. Nothing about him suggests that he is involved in such an exotic trade, he might as well be a pharmacist or a librarian.

Holmgren points out another dealer—a dapper gentleman with a crisp gray mustache who could be mistaken for an architect or a corporate attorney.

Norris Dominick. You never know what he wants, but he pays top dollar.

Dominick seems to be ignoring the auction. Expensively dressed in a tailored black pinstripe suit, convinced of his own success, arms folded and lips pursed, he gazes dustily through Piglett's rustic performance. Muhlbach notes that he hasn't bothered to get a bidding card.

Holmgren has located another. Fourth row, turtleneck sweater. Arthur Guy. His thing is pre-Columbian. He's got a gallery in the Village. Remember those TV commercials where the secret agent was smoking a little cigar. That was Guy. He used to be a model.

Muhlbach straightens up for a look at the former secret agent. Not much can be seen except the back of his head. Next to him sits a red-haired goddess with a superb profile. They aren't paying any attention to each other but there's no doubt that they belong together, just as surely as the Jalisco couple.

Holmgren identifies a few regulars while the auction continues.

That fat lady in the sixth row with the cigarette holder—she's into paperweights. You won't believe this, Muhlbach, but she's got a penthouse full of paperweights. Stay away from her. All she talks about is paperweights. Baccarat. Lily-of-the-valley. Talk your ears off. And the fellow with the pipe and the canvas jacket. That's Roska or Prohaska— one of those hunky names. Retired paint salesman. Nice old bird, born in Warsaw. His thing is moccasins. You couldn't give him a paperweight. But moccasins? Could be he knows more about moccasins than anybody in the world.

Who are the pre-Columbian collectors?

Holmgren surveys the audience.

There's one. Over there in dungarees leaning against the wall. He never sits down, always leans against something. He's into pre-Columbian but he also goes for Northwest Coast wood carving. He likes cedar boxes. Haida. Kwakiutl. Any kind of cedar box and he starts acting nervous, especially boxes with abalone inlay. Don't talk to him. He's nuts. Also, the bald guy in the corner wiping his mouth with a handkerchief—sometimes he bids on pre-Columbian jade but his real thing is rugs. He's got a Two Gray Hills the Smithsonian wants. He told the Smithsonian they could have his wife but not his Two Gray Hills.

Holmgren stops. Piglett's son is holding up a small black plate, quite attractive, with a matte design.

Maria, he whispers. That'll go for a bundle. At least a hundred.

Muhlbach remembers the plate. Donna would like it and he had thought about offering a couple of dollars. He glances at the catalogue:

San Ildefonso black ware. Maria Martinez.

Holmgren is correct not only about the potter but about the price. It goes for one hundred and fifty.

Congratulations, friend, says Piglett to the buyer, you got yourself a real bargain. If you want to sell that plate for one fifty just bring it back. A year from now I might give you three times that much.

Then a small brown pot signed by Grace Medicine Flower from the Santa Clara pueblo sells for almost as much. A pot by Joseph Lonewolf—simply a pot with a green turtle painted on one side—brings two hundred.

Holmgren has begun to tug his beard and suck at his teeth. The Yurok basket will soon be up.

Muhlbach gets ready. With the card on his lap he waits tensely while several rugs are sold. Then a clam shell necklace. Then a pair of buckskin leggings with silver bells. Finally they get to the rare Yurok half-twist overlay.

The basket collectors are enthusiastic: Thirty. Thirty-five. Forty. Forty-five?

He waves the card.

Fifty?

In the front row somebody gestures.

Now fifty-five? A museum quality Yurok. Who'll go fifty-five?

Apparently somebody makes a bid because Piglett jumps to sixty. This seems like too much, but it's what Holmgren has authorized. All right, sixty.

Sixty-five?

Muhlbach scans the audience. It's obvious why Holmgren chose to sit in the last row. You can keep an eye on everybody. He notices that the lady in the Persian lamb coat has turned around to stare at him.

Piglett gets a bid for sixty-five and Muhlbach relaxes. It's all over.

Seventy? Seventy dollars for this fine Yurok? Worth five times that much. Who'll go seventy?

He feels a quick nudge in the ribs and glances at Holmgren in disbelief. Seventy dollars for a wicker basket?

Last call. Seventy? Once. Twice.

Yes! Up goes the card. This is absurd, he tells himself. Everybody in the room must think I'm a fool.

Piglett resumes chanting: Seventy-five? Seventy-five?

The lady in the Persian lamb has turned around to stare at him again. She looks narrowly at Holmgren. She is not sure, but she is suspicious. In back of those ugly nouveau riche spectacles her flat brown eyes twinkle with profound malice. And all at once Muhlbach understands that he has made an enemy. In fact, although she doesn't collect pre-Columbian, when the Olmec comes up she may buy it.

Somebody has offered seventy-five for the Yurok. Holmgren wags his head. Too much. Even so, there is one further bid. The basket finally goes for eighty.

Piglett's next treasure is the weather-whitened skull of a bighorn sheep. A young man wearing a velveteen blouse and his hair in a ponytail thinks enough of it to pay sixteen dollars.

Holmgren chuckles. Wes found that beside the road.

Next is a rawhide whip. Four dollars. Then a prospector's canteen. Then a Chiricahua drum used by Geronimo, according to Piglett. An assayer's scale from the Sacramento Wells Fargo office. A pair of leather saddle bags. A gourd carved and painted to resemble a bird. A solid bronze lizard. More Navajo and Chimayo rugs.

No. 128. Cellophane bag of turquoise nuggets. It goes for three dollars.

No. 129. Huge Mexican jadeite mask. Very rare.

Jeff, Piglett says to his son, hold that mask high enough so the folks can get a good look. All right, who's going to offer one thousand dollars for a huge jade mask? And that's not onyx or soapstone. That's real jade, I guarantee it. Anybody tells you that's not real Mexican jade I'll give you your thousand back, plus interest. All right, who'll give five hundred?

Nobody.

Three hundred? One hundred? Well, who'll give ten dollars? Sure you will! You know you will. Now twenty. And now thirty? Sure you will! And forty down here in front. Now fifty? Fifty on the side. Sixty? And now seventy? Seventy in front. Now eighty, who'll give eighty?

After a long pause he gets eighty. Then eighty-five. Another pause.

Ninety! Thank you. Ninety-five?

Nobody will offer that much. Piglett hates to let it go. This is a bargain, the chance of a lifetime.

I'm going to let you have one chance at ninety-two fifty.

Muhlbach holds up his card.

Ninety-five anybody? Once. Don't let this get away, you'll be sorry. Twice. Last chance on the biggest jade mask you'll ever see. Ninety-five?

Then just for an instant while Piglett is jotting down his number Muhlbach becomes the most important person in the room. People turn around to contemplate him.

No. 130. Frame of arrowheads. All right, Jeff, let the folks see it. I found some of those arrowheads myself. We were in Texas after a big rainstorm and me and the kids and Dixie filled almost a cigar box full of arrowheads in less than three hours. Who'll give twenty dollars?

No. 131. Battle Mountain spiderweb turquoise bracelet. Who'll give a sawbuck to start things off? You folks are sitting on your hands.

No. 132. Orange coral necklace. Long branch. Rare.

No. 133. Genuine old Navajo rug. 1910–1915. Ganado red.

No. 134. Plastic box of fire opals.

No. 135. Authentic early American leg irons. They had these irons on Billy the Kid, but he got loose and you know what happened. Who'll give a thousand dollars for the leg irons Billy Bonney wore? Well, how about five dollars? Who's going to start it off?

No. 136. Bronze bell. This is the victory bell they rang after the battle of Pueblo. 1811 is the date I can read on it. Those revolutionaries used to make these bells out of captured gold and silver, so you figure it out. Who'll give ten dollars? Did I say ten dollars? That's not enough money. Let's hear it, Jeff.

Jeff, inscrutable, sucks his toothpick and rings the bell.

No. 137. Metate and pestle. Guatemala. Volcanic stone. A big one. If you buy it and don't pick it up after the auction we're going to ship it to you airmail. Special delivery. C.O.D.

No. 138. Framed drawing by Mary Cunliffe O'Brien. Here's a winner. Any of you know who Mary Cunliffe O'Brien is? She's Dade O'Brien's wife—the famous western artist. She's not married to Dade anymore, she's married to Rembrandt. Who'll give three dollars for this authentic signed O'Brien?

Muhlbach listens without understanding. He feels stunned. Having spent practically one hundred dollars he now remembers that he was not going to buy anything. But at the same time he has acquired a masterpiece of the extinct Olmec civilization— which seems incredible. Why did the dealers let it get away? Didn't they recognize it? And what about those pre-Columbian collectors in the audience? This is very strange, he thinks, absently pinching the lobe of his ear. Very strange indeed. A logical explanation, of course, is that the mask is a fake. But I know it isn't. And besides, the thing is jade, so this doesn't make sense. This simply does not make sense.

He stares at the bizarre assortment of artifacts trickling from the banquet tables. A bone-handled sheath knife. A stuffed badger. Antlers mounted on a varnished wooden plaque. Bolo ties. A machete in a rotten leather scabbard. A powder horn. A fossilized walrus tusk. Blankets. Wampum. But none of it means anything. His brain streaked with unanswerable questions, his eyes out of focus, he sits erect and motionless on the uncomfortable metal chair.

Piglett is ready for the quartet of ersatz Mayans.

Muhlbach blinks. Yes, there they are—splotched with ink and stained with shoe polish—as new as the souvenirs at the Albuquerque airport.

Guy and his Irish beauty, whispering over the catalogue, pay no attention. Dominick opens a silver cigarette case, selects one and calmly lights it.

The fake Mayans sell for a few dollars apiece.

More jewelry and rugs. A necklace of eagle talons. A Northwest Coast stone ax—a slave killer, according to the catalogue. Squirrel skin gloves. A rusty harpoon. Snow-shoes.

Muhlbach consults his list. The Jalisco couple will soon be up. He decides that it should go for quite a lot less than the Olmec. It is, after all, not jade but clay. Twenty or thirty dollars. Forty at the most.

Piglett stops talking as his son starts to lift the Jalisco couple with one hand.

Easy with that. Let's use both hands, Jeff.

Arthur Guy is now attentive. Dominick taps the ash from his cigarette as though nothing could interest him less. Just the same, something is not quite right about Dominick's attitude. They're after it, Muhlbach thinks.

Piglett resumes his spiel:

Here we go. You've been waiting for this baby. You pre-Columbian collectors take a good look. This is a honey. You dealers know what it is. This is one of the finest Jalisco items I've ever handled. From the west coast of Mexico. Third or fourth century. Maybe even earlier, I don't know. Nobody knows for sure how old these pieces are. The Mexican government has cracked down and a lot of people are in Chihuahua jails for trying to smuggle these across the border. There was a fellow killed last spring trying to ford the Rio Grande with a load of pre-Columbian. A few years ago you couldn't give these things away. Mexican ranchers used to find these idols and set them up on fence posts and use them for target practice. Probably shot up a million dollars' worth. Today they're shooting themselves. Lift that piece higher, Jeff.

Piglett mops his face with a handkerchief.

I tell you it's hot under these lights. Now let's get busy and sell this thing before Jeff gives out on me. Pre-Columbian couple from the state of Jalisco. Guaranteed authentic. If this piece was standing on a pedestal in one of those Madison Avenue galleries where the salesman wears a necktie you'd expect to pay a thousand dollars. Maybe more. I don't know what they charge. They won't let me in the front door of those galleries the way I'm dressed. Norris Dominick down here—if I want to see what he's got for sale in that fancy place of his I got to go around to the back so he can sneak me in. All right, Norris won't bat an eye, but he knows what this piece is worth. Raoul and Art and Clyde and Mrs. Lowenfeld and the rest of you dealers—you know what it's worth. All right, get a good look and don't let this baby slip away for a few dollars. You'll be sorry later on. Jeff, get one of your lazy brothers to hold that piece if you're all wore out. Now here we go. This item is on consignment. There's a reserve price of five hundred dollars, so who wants to start it off at five twenty-five for a museum quality joined pair from the state of Jalisco?

Thank you. Five twenty-five down front. Now five fifty? Five fifty. Now five seventy-five? It's worth a hundred times that much. You dealers won't let this get away for five fifty. You're too smart for that.

Bidding stops at five hundred and seventy-five.

Piglett tries to squeeze out a little more. Ten dollars from somebody in the front row, then another ten from a woman who doesn't look as if she could afford it.

Dixie and me and the kids thank you, ma'am. Five ninety-five. Now six hundred. Six hundred?

Guy is still attentive. Dominick, too, must be interested because Piglett often glances at him. Muhlbach sits with the numbered card upside down on his lap, arms folded in absolute disbelief.

Piglett speaks to him directly:

You collectors better wake up. Tomorrow you'll decide you want this piece and it'll cost you a fortune. If you don't believe me, just find out the prices in those expensive galleries with a carpet on the floor. You couldn't touch a Jalisco couple like this for six hundred dollars and I'll guarantee it. And I'll bet you the dealers in the audience will tell you the same thing.

Muhlbach shakes his head.

All right, don't say I didn't warn you. Six hundred? Once. Who'll give six hundred? Twice. Final call. Don't let this baby slip away.

At the last instant he finds another card. Sure you will!

Twenty dollars later he gives up.

Sold! Art, you got yourself a bargain. Lay it aside, Jeff, so your mother don't trip over it and send the whole family to the poorhouse. Now, what have we got next? Mesa Verde pot. Probably about the twelfth century. Not a real big one but a good one. You ask around in Durango or Gallup and they'll charge you fifty dollars for a pot like this. It's got a chip out of the rim and a little tiny hole in the bottom you can't hardly notice. Who's going to give twenty dollars for this authentic Mesa Verde?

Holmgren is ready to leave. A few more baskets will be sold but none that he wants. He smiles uncertainly.

See you at the next auction, I guess. Let me know how that mask turns out.

He walks toward the exit with head bowed, empty-handed, always defeated. Lady Luck has misplaced Holmgren's address. He needs a belt, either that or his trousers are too long, because the cuffs trail shabbily along the floor. Muhlbach, watching him disappear, feels an unexplainable sense of regret.

But that remark about the mask—what did he mean? Well, what he meant is obvious. He suspects it may be a fake. He's wrong, of course. But just the same, why weren't any dealers bidding on it?

At that moment, as though suggesting an answer to the question, Arthur Guy stands up. So does the Irish beauty. They make their way to the aisle and walk hand in hand toward the old-fashioned painted tin cash box where Dixie presides. A few people already have checked out and now with most of the merchandise sold a line is starting to form. Guy takes his place at the end. Dealers evidently have no special privilege.

Well, why hesitate and worry? Guy should know. Why not ask? Seize the dealer by the horns. Look here, Mr. Guy, what about the mask? Is it Olmec or was I swindled?

Muhlbach stands up. I dislike doing this, he thinks. It's presumptuous.

The lady in the Persian lamb coat is also heading for the cash box so he is obliged to walk quickly. He manages to get there first, but it was close enough to be embarrassing. She rewards his speed with a viper-like stare, the rhinestones of her spectacles flashing dangerously.

One by one the buyers carry off their acquisitions:

An old man with a Navajo chief's blanket.

Schoolgirls with turquoise jewelry.

A fat woman with the Hopi kachina.

Fetishes, spurs, hides, rugs, silver buckles. Some of the purchases seem appropriate, some don't.

Muhlbach waits for a convenient moment, but Guy clings to the lady's hand. Under the circumstances it would be awkward to tap him on the shoulder. At the table, however, he lets go long enough to write a check.

I beg your pardon, Muhlbach begins, and rapidly explains.

Guy, instead of answering, maneuvers for time by introducing the lady. Maureen. Maureen has no last name. From this distance she doesn't look quite so youthful. She must be approaching forty. And those expectant green eyes—motionless as a pair of spiders—show signs of deadly experience.

By now Guy has decided how to respond. They were just going to the coffee shop for a sandwich. Would Muhlbach care to come along?

Not a word about the mask, although of course he might have something important to say. He might want to explain why he didn't bid on it.

Yes, I would. Thank you. Suppose I join you there after I pick up the stone.

Arthur Guy smiles. The green-eyed goddess smiles. Hand in hand they stroll away.

After I pick up the stone, Muhlbach mutters to himself while writing a check. 'After I pick up the stone.' Lord, what an imbecilic way to express it. No wonder they smiled. They must be laughing aloud. They won't be in the coffee shop. I wouldn't be there myself if some fool tried to insinuate himself as I just did.

Dixie apologizes for the fact that they don't have any wrapping paper, not even a sack.

Now this is absurd, Muhlbach thinks, I can't walk around holding a jade mask. But luckily, with a little shoving, it can be forced into an overcoat pocket.

So, carrying his gloves and homburg, the mask weighing against his thigh like a holstered .45, he strides along the mica-speckled corridor, down a flight of Chinese blue steps, past the imitation walnut reception desk and through the trellis of plastic flowers to the frosted glass doors guarding the coffee shop.

The doors burst apart and hesitate, trembling with eagerness.

Inside the coffee shop he glances around. Guy and his beauty won't be there.

But they are. And they wave, both of them, at exactly the same moment.

I'm afraid I've imposed on you, he begins.

Not in the least.

I suppose you examined the mask during the preview.

Yes.

Then of course you wouldn't need a second look.

No.

Guy's response isn't encouraging.

I might as well be frank and tell you that I'm an amateur. This prehistoric art business is, so to speak, altogether new.

His lady is less sympathetic:

We thought so. We were watching you, Mr. Muhlbach, and when you squinted at the mask we were positive.

He looks at her critically. Who is she? Maybe an art teacher. Maybe she has a little collection.

A derisive smile curls her full moist lips.

Scratching the mask with your key. Scrubbing it with your handkerchief. Honestly, Mr. Muhlbach! Those 'foolproof' tests reveal more about the person than about the artifact. In the gallery we get the tasters and the sniffers and the mystics and Heaven knows what else. Arthur insists we let them have their fun because it's harmless. Except the scratchers —we do put a stop to that. In regard to your mask, though, it scarcely matters.

Are you implying that it's a fake?

Authentication can be difficult. With stone particularly. As you may or may not know, the Olmecs colored their sculpture. We very often find traces of hematite and red mercuric sulphide on Olmec jades. However, that ochre stain in the eye sockets and rictus of your mask—that would be a modern dye. Acetone should remove it.

Guy completes her statement as though it were his own:

With terra cotta or wood you have a chance. Time does things to a wood surface which are almost impossible to duplicate. Then you have your various lab tests—carbon fourteen and the like. With clay you have your calcium deposits and manganese dioxide and so forth. But with stone it's tricky. Tricky as hell. Take it to the Natural History museum. Show it to Gordon Ekholm. Or take it up to the Indian museum and ask Fred Dockstader to look at it.

Muhlbach blinks in surprise. Ekholm. Dockstader. Are these men accessible to the public? Guy apparently knows them, or at least has talked to them. What an idea. It's worth thinking about, though one might also think about requesting an interview with the Pope.

Thank you for the suggestion. I may possibly do that. But now in regard to style, what could you tell me? Did you notice any stylistic mistakes?

The dealer takes a swallow of coffee. He strokes the tip of his nose, he bites his upper lip. Then he asks to see the mask again.

Muhlbach manages to extract it and places it on a paper napkin in the middle of the table. For some reason—maybe the fluorescent light, or the fact that it appears to have been mounted on colored paper— the mask looks less convincing.

Guy seems to be observing it from miles above. Obviously he regards it as a contaminated object. Maureen looks down on it with cynical green eyes, those evocative pink lips taut with displeasure.

Guy leans back in the booth. Wrong. Everything's wrong.

Maureen shrugs. Mechanical. Simply mechanical.

Muhlbach begins to feel annoyed by their habit of speaking alternately. Furthermore, these generalities aren't helpful. How about a specific answer?

The chin, for instance. Would that chin be Olmec or Toltec? After all, the mask does resemble Olmec masks in the books. As a matter of fact, it is almost indistinguishable from the Tenango del Valle master-piece.

Guy shakes his head. He mutters about form, about volume. Nothing really quite works. The edges aren't right. The whole thing is wrong.

Guerrero? Maureen suggests.

Could be, Guy answers.

Ignacio?

I was thinking the same.

Muhlbach interrupts. Who is Ignacio?

Ignacio Cedral. His carvings usually are smaller than this, and he doesn't often use jadeite because it's so hard. But stylistically—stylistically this does look like one of Ignacio's products.

Maureen furnishes a little extra information:

He lives near Chilpancingo, we've been told, and has a number of apprentices. Some of the work isn't half bad. Last year we were offered an absolutely delightful steatite jaguar. Unfortunately, Ignacio has a passion for detail and he simply could not resist the temptation to give his cat some whiskers. It was a terrible faux pas.

I don't believe one word of this, Muhlbach thinks. Not a word. Are you telling me that not only is the mask a fake but you know who carved it?

Maureen replies pleasantly:

If you know Fragonard you will recognize Fragon-ard.

True enough. But there is a great difference be-tween a Fragonard and the work of some provincial stone carver.

That's hardly the point.

Well, she's right, of course. Familiarity with an artist's style is what she was talking about.

Try the museum, Guy insists. We could be dead wrong. We've got a granite ceremonial ax in the gallery that worries hell out of me. It should be late classic or early post-classic from Guatemala, but I don't like it. I've gone over it a hundred times and I've shown it to everybody. No consensus.

Right there, Muhlbach thinks angrily, we have the same damned vague guesswork. Probabilities. Possibilities. Why don't these people come up with definite answers? Nobody gives you a flat yes or no. Except that young anthropologist in Albuquerque— he knew what he believed. Or maybe he was wrong too.

And the longer he considers the situation the more exasperated he becomes. Other businesses by comparison are childishly simple. So many bolts of cloth at so much per bolt. Such and such a premium over a specified number of years. But these pre-Columbian people with their interminable doubts and qualifications.

He drums on the table top:

Mr. Guy, I would like to ask an awkward question. Just how do you authenticate the objects you offer for sale?

If I could explain in a couple of words, I would.

Maureen interrupts:

I have a one-word answer for you, Mr. Muhlbach. Experience.

I check things out with Gordon and Fred if I'm not satisfied.

Don't forget Carlos.

We hash it over with everybody. Get as many viewpoints as we can.

Arthur is terribly cautious. He abhors fakes.

That's commendable. But tell me, in cases of doubt does the museum supply a categoric answer?

One in a while. As a rule they supply nothing more than an opinion.

I'm getting nowhere, Muhlbach says to himself. If these people know what they're talking about they certainly keep it a secret.

He turns to Guy:

You bought the Jalisco, unless I'm mistaken.

Right.

For love rather than profit, Maureen remarks. Arthur, you did pay too much.

Norris wanted it.

Who else? I do mistrust him.

Muhlbach looks back and forth. Who is the 'him' that she mistrusts?

Oh, she answers with a wave of contempt, that huckster. He draws bids from the clouds. You've got to be so careful or you end up bidding against yourself. If that man thought he could cheat God he wouldn't hesitate.

Then why do business with him? Aren't you asking for trouble?

He called about the Jalisco. He does that only if he's brought an exceptional piece.

Are you sure it's authentic?

She waits for Guy to answer.

I'll go over it tomorrow or the next day—whenever Wes delivers it—but it looks good. Norris and I talked about it. The piece has some unusual features for the Etzatlán site, which is pretty far north, but that doesn't make me suspicious. No, I feel it's okay.

Maureen continues:

Since you were anxious to obtain a bona fide Olmec you should have taken the bowl.

Several bowls were auctioned. He remembers two or three but none that might have been Olmec.

She describes it: five inches in diameter, cylindrical, ivory-colored with a crudely scratched geometric design.

Ah, yes. He remembers picking up a cracked dirty white bowl, but the catalogue didn't list it as Olmec.

It was a very late example, says Guy. The shape was typical and the glyph is one we come across pretty frequently on Olmec ware. Michoacan and

Veracruz pottery sometimes has a similar glyph, but there it only serves as a starting point for elaboration—cross-checks and zigzags to fill up the surrounding panel area. Outside the Olmec culture we don't usually come across such a simple pattern, so the design in conjunction with the size and that characteristic off-white color would make it fairly definite.

You could have snapped it up for next to nothing, Maureen adds.

Why didn't the catalogue list it as Olmec?

Because Mr. Piglett, who has only the sketchiest knowledge of pre-Columbian, couldn't identify it.

All right, Muhlbach thinks. But assuming it was a bargain, why didn't Guy bid on it?

The dealer explains that there isn't much of a market for bowls. A collector looking for an Olmec will almost always ask for one of those plump slant-eyed babies. Or a jade, if he's rich enough. Then, too, the bowl Piglett was offering did have a crack, which further limits the salability.

Did you pick up anything except the Jalisco?

The rest was garbage.

Maureen agrees.

But that couple! Guy exclaims, kissing his finger-tips like a Latin.

'For love rather than profit.' Yes, now it's clear. Guy bought the Jalisco not simply for resale but because he wanted it. What a pastiche of aesthetics, art and commerce.

Muhlbach glances at the clock on the wall.

I should be going. Thank you both. It was good of you to give me an opinion about the mask.

Have Ekholm check it out.

I might. In any case, I appreciate what you've told me and I hope I haven't taken too much of your time.

Oh, nonsense! Maureen remarks. Arthur is a frightfully poor businessman but where pre-Columbian art is concerned he always has time to talk about it.

Just by chance, would either of you be acquainted with a screenwriter named Claude Varda?

Dear Claude! Yes indeed, Mr. Muhlbach. We know him. Every dealer in New York knows him. I do think he visits the gallery merely to complain about prices. He cannot get used to the idea that the days of buying things for a few pesos at an archaeological site are over. He calls us robbers— *ladrones*. Are you and Claude friends?

I'm not sure. Though I must admit I share his feeling about pre-Columbian prices, if that Jalisco is any sample.

Oh, I hope you won't turn into another Claude. He does become furious. He swears at us and stamps around and insists he'll never visit the gallery again. But prices are not coming down, you know. With contemporary art it's such a guess—the artist may just be in vogue. I feel so sorry for those collectors who poured money into the works of yesterday's genius. But with old masters, whether they lived in Venice or Tlatilco, you make a solid investment.

I dare say you're right. I have no doubt it's a better investment than the stock market. These days, at least.

This day or any day, Mr. Muhlbach.

Guy plucks a card from his wallet. Here. Stop by and see us.

I will.

Maureen watches him stuff the mask once more into his pocket.

If it's any consolation, that actually is jade. You might be able to get your money back by selling it to a lapidary.

Is she trying to be helpful? Or was there a trace of poison in that comment? Well, it stings, no matter what she had in mind. And despite what she thinks—or what they both think—the mask might be authentic.

Goodnight.

Goodnight. They smile and nod like puppets. In another moment they'll be holding hands.

Strange couple. Guy is handsome enough to be mistaken for a celebrity. But he doesn't radiate anything. He's bland, less forceful and probably less intelligent than his calculating lady. How intimate they seem and yet how dissimilar they are, though they both give the impression of being narcissistic. He reeks of shaving lotion and she—well, nothing. No perfume. No invitation.

But that's neither here nor there, Muhlbach reminds himself as he leaves the motel. All I'm concerned about is the extent to which Mr. Arthur Guy knows this pre-Columbian business. I just wonder if he might be wrong about the mask. Was he being polite or is he really uncertain?

At home under the congenial glow of lamplight the Olmec begins to look less spurious. The carved face seems genuinely bestial, rudimentary, primitive. One might even describe it as barbaric. Turning it over and over in his hands, Muhlbach studies the laboriously cut stone. What a tremendous amount of work. Why would a skilled craftsman, no matter how poor, work such a long time for a few dollars?

Guy could indeed be wrong. Yes, Arthur Guy and the beautiful astringent lady with no last name might very well be mistaken. Despite the fact that he's a professional and she—whoever or whatever she is—knows more than I do, they just might have slipped up. Experience isn't everything. What about sensibility? Yes, and I certainly have a keen eye. Nobody's ever accused me of being imperceptive. Besides, Guy wasn't dogmatic. If anything, he sounded doubtful. Show it to somebody else, he said. All right, if he's no more positive than that, I will.

ON a snowy Friday afternoon with the mask again stuffed into his pocket, Muhlbach marches through the doors of the Natural History museum and submits his request. The woman at the desk listens courteously, makes a telephone call and then informs him that Dr. Ekholm is occupied. However, Mr. Sanchez could look at the item.

Well, Mr. Sanchez may not be famous, but if he's associated with the museum he must be competent. All right, where do I find Mr. Sanchez?

Fifth floor. Take the elevator. And put this on your lapel, she adds, giving him a button. That area is not open to the public.

A few minutes later Muhlbach is wandering around the fifth floor, annoyed with himself for not having listened more attentively. The problem now is to locate Sanchez, whose office is locked. Where would he be?

The door to another office is half open. He peeps in. Behind a rolltop desk an elderly gentleman with white hair is reading a magazine.

Sanchez? Right down the way.

Muhlbach explains that the office seems to be locked.

Ah! It is, is it? Well, he was going to Vermont this weekend so he must have left.

But the receptionist just spoke with him.

She did, did she? Then he should be here. Ask around. He can't be far.

Muhlbach continues along the hall. Nobody is in sight. All at once he hears typing, but the noise stops before he can identify the room. At the opposite end of the hall a door closes and he immediately turns around, but whoever was there has disappeared. An instant later another door opens, a young girl wearing a Norwegian ski sweater steps out, clutches her head and hurries toward him with a distracted expression.

She's mad, he thinks. Totally mad. However, she might know where Sanchez can be found. He begins to explain the situation while the girl stares up at him with her mouth agape, brushing repeatedly at a lock of hair that falls in front of one eye.

But I don't work in the museum, she says at last. I'm just trying to find Miss Pellegrini. Could you tell me where she is? They told me she was in this department.

I don't know. I'm sorry.

Please!

You don't seem to understand. I don't work here either. I'm trying to locate a Mr. Sanchez.

But I've got to find her. I'm not kidding, it's important.

I can't help you! Muhlbach replies more sharply than he intended.

Then at the sound of footsteps he glances up. A man in a laboratory smock is approaching. Almost certainly this would be Sanchez.

No. No, but if you run you might catch him at the elevator.

Muhlbach dashes along the hall and turns a corner in time to watch the elevator door bump shut.

It's possible, of course, that Sanchez was not aboard that particular elevator. Or, even if he was, he might return. But it now seems plain to Muhlbach that he is destined never to catch up with Sanchez. After thinking about this he shrugs and starts back toward the office where the white-haired gentleman was reading.

He, at least, stays put. In fact he doesn't appear to have moved. He peers across the top of his spectacles in mild surprise.

Ah. Sanchez has gone, has he? Just as I thought. That's a shame.

I was wondering if I could leave the mask here. Perhaps you could give it to him when he comes in on Monday.

Oh, he'll not likely be in before Tuesday. Then, too, that would be irregular, you know.

I see.

But perhaps I could. I've been here some time. I doubt they'll discharge me. Yes. Yes, set your item there on the table. I'll get it to Sanchez the first of the week.

Muhlbach puts the mask beside a rectangular wire basket overflowing with papers.

Sorry to be so much trouble.

No trouble. No trouble at all.

When should I come back?

Friday, I should guess. I can't say what Sanchez is up to, you know. But I should guess Friday ought to do the job.

Fine. I'll stop by a week from today.

And your name, sir?

Muhlbach.

Very well, Mr. Muhlbach. Good day.

So, if things haven't worked out perfectly. at least the mask is in the museum. Sanchez will have plenty of time to study it. Yes, there's that to consider. He'll have a chance to go over it carefully. Not catching him may be a blessing in disguise. He won't feel rushed. He might even have a few other people examine it. In fact, he just might discuss the mask with Dr. Ekholm, Muhlbach thinks, and claps his hands.

He begins to feel a mysterious excitement, somewhat like the excitement of joining a lodge or a country club. It seems to him that he is about to be initiated. What will they say next Friday? Assuming the mask turns out to be authentic, they will want to know how he happened to discover it. And what a coup if he should casually remark that several dealers were at the auction—several of the most respected dealers in New York—and not one spotted the mask as genuine.

It occurs to him as he steps out of the elevator that he might have a quick look at the museum's pre-Columbian exhibit. Five minutes till closing. Well, five minutes is better than nothing. He steps back into the elevator.

Mexican primitive art?

Second floor. To your left.

Next week, he thinks while striding past a group of children looking at stuffed birds, I'll try to get here earlier. Maybe I could arrange to leave the office by three-thirty.

Directly ahead is the entrance:

MEXICO AND CENTRAL AMERICA

He starts around the room, pausing a moment at the rainbow charts of prehistoric migrations. Yes, get here early enough to spend some time on these details.

In a display case filled with Olmec sculpture is the famous Kunz ax. Not a reproduction. The thing itself. Gleaming blue-gray jadeite almost a foot long. Incredible. And nearby is that wooden ceremonial mask—the only wooden Olmec object known—with slits for eyes and a leper's jaw, reputedly found in a cave high on a cliff of the Cañon de la Mano near Iguala. The forehead and the cheeks originally were inlaid with jade. Fragments of polished jade still adhere to the surface. Date uncertain but approximately a millennium before Christ. And a monkey pendant—not a terribly serious monkey, though no one can be sure what amused these enigmatic people.

After a glance at his watch Muhlbach hurries toward the next cabinet.

Remojadas ceramics. Laughing faces, infants, gate figures with that familiar resinous black paint. He bends down to read the description and congratulates himself. Central Veracruz. Proto-classic. Yes, just as I suspected.

And a whiteware Nopiloa lady sporting a marvelous waterfowl headdress. She's wearing some sort of animal or reptile skin with pointed teeth or scales slung around her neck and fastened with brooches. Late classic. Fine creamy gray color. A lady anyone would love to possess.

And against the wall one of those giant Olmec heads like a boulder on a platform. It must weigh twenty tons. He approaches with a sense of respect, almost of deference, and decides to squander a minute on the colossus.

The Olmec head, however, is not an original.

This information spoils the impact. He turns away with a feeling of resentment. There's no reason one should not gaze respectfully at a plaster cast, but somehow, knowing that the head is a reproduction has lessened its grandeur. One could, of course, read the description before looking at an object, which would take care of any misapprehensions. Yet wouldn't that knowledge affect one's judgment? Well, what began as a simple visit seems to be developing philosophic tendrils.

I'd like to sit down, he thinks. Those benches aren't exactly inviting, but what I really would like to do is just sit here and meditate and look around.

Ah! The Mayans!

He starts across the room but five minutes are up. A guard appears.

On route to the exit he pauses for a moment at the

Nayarit display. Some pathetic human quality is epitomized by the commonplace villagers—by their musical instruments, houses and barking dogs. How unaffected these people look in their homely urban clothing, how mortal and how tragic compared to the fluorescent plenipotentiaries from Teotihuacán and Chiapas and Mitla and El Tajín.

But time's up, he says to himself, and I've collected impressions enough for one day. Furthermore, I have no idea where this adventure is leading, though I do know I'm being led. In any event, we'll see what we'll see next week.

Walking thoughtfully down the museum steps he concludes that some additional reading might be advisable before his audience with Sanchez. It wouldn't hurt to learn as much as possible about the Olmecs.

All right, he mutters half aloud while waiting for a signal to change. Books. I ought to get more books. Yes, and a jeweler's glass. Definitely I should have a jeweler's glass.

In an optical shop he selects an imported stainless steel Carton, a precise professional instrument very much like Quimby's, with two lenses that swivel neatly in and out of the handle. Fifteen-power on one side. Ten-power on the other.

From the optical shop to the Fifth Avenue bookstores where he spends an hour looking at pictures of ball courts, ruined temples, stone calendars and bark paper codices, and sampling the erudite text:

Whether in basalt or jade, the Olmec style has a deceptive simplicity. Its apparent naturalism appeals immediately to the eye but soon troubles the mind with a disquieting sense of meaning not understood. Any of the colossal heads would have this effect because of its size alone. Who can help wondering whether Olmec sculptors humanized their god into this brooding but beneficent form, or whether they served rulers who were American counterparts of Ramses the Great? (His grandiose portraits may have been staring out over the Nile for less than a century when the first huge head was carved at San Lorenzo.) Precious material lends mystery to some of the small carvings . . .

The impact of ancient Olmec art upon the modern beholder, nevertheless, is not entirely a matter of size, preciousness, or mystery. It comes also from a persuasively literal mode of symbolization. Realistic human and animal elements are often joined together in a single figure, but with such grace and assurance that the unreal seems believable.

In the Mixtec codices it is possible to read when a king was born, when he died, whom he married, what his victories and titles were, the places he conquered and by whom he was succeeded. The lives of many extraordinary personages are recorded in detail, such as Five Reed, the reformer of the calendar, and his still more famous son, the great conqueror Eight Deer Jaguarclaw. The latter's life is described in detail from his birth in 1011 and his investiture as chieftain in the imperial city of Tula (in a ceremonial which included the ritual perforation of the septum of his nose with an eagle talon or jaguar claw so that he could wear a ruler's distinguishing nose ornament) to his death in 1063. The codices tell of his wives, the Lady Six Monkeys and the Lady Thirteen Serpents . . .

Although Mezcala figures and Chontal masks appear in late Aztec tombs, these imported pieces may have come as tribute exacted from Guerrero residents, who had to loot older tombs to fulfill the demand, much as they do today to fill the demand of the international art market. The earliest Mezcala figures that can be dated were unearthed beneath a wall built at the beginning of the classic period in the Central Mexican metropolis of Teotihuacán . . .

Frequently found in Oaxaca are small, amulet-size stone figurines of gods and ancestors which locally are quite appropriately called *peñates* (the Latin term for household gods). They represent squatting or standing men, their features incised with straight-line and circular or semicircular drilled cuts typical of this period's mass-production techniques. Some are carved in a very summary fashion indeed, while others show fine detailing. Each has a small drilled perforation in back through which a string could be passed. The finest of them are carved out of jade or onyx, while others are cut out of more common stones. They bear a striking resemblance to the small Tiki ancestor figurines of the Marquesas Islands . . .

The ceramic of the Chicanel period is decorated with negative or resist paint, with incised lines after the slip was applied, as well as with grooves and appliqué. There is a greater variety of forms than in the Mamom period. These include four-legged vessels with conical, cylindrical, and teat-shaped supports, and bowls with low annular bases. A subsequent formative phase, absent at Uaxactún, was discovered at Holmul in Guatemala . . .

At last he starts home with a heavy package for his library, and arrives too late. Supper is over.

Good evening, Mrs. Grunthe, good evening! How are we this evening?

Mrs. Grunthe is not pleased.

But with so many splendid books, as well as a jeweler's glass, the housekeeper's disposition hardly matters. Besides, Mrs. Grunthe is almost always displeased.

I'll just have some soup and a sandwich. Don't go to a lot of trouble.

Oh, you can be sure of that! Soup and a sandwich. Coming home this hour of the night. The devil himself would be more considerate. Mrs. Grunthe, muttering, plods toward the kitchen.

Otto and Donna are curious about the glass. At the sight of more books filled with ugly pictures they turn aside; books make them fear that another dreadful boring lecture may be coming up. He reassures them. Once was enough. But here now—just take a look through this. Let me show you how to hold it.

Otto and Donna are fascinated. By the time they finish playing with the new toy practically everything in the living room has been scrutinized. But at last they're in bed and the house is quiet, except for Mrs. Grunthe noisily demonstrating her exasperation among the pots and pans.

Muhlbach takes the Taos lord from his throne on the mantel.

Ten times enlarged, the miniature aristocrat looks more unapproachable than ever. Woe to the common man. At this tribunal you'd better hope Quetzalcóatl intervenes on your behalf.

Fifteen times enlarged, not much can be distinguished except dim gray-blue craters and gorges, mountains of the moon—shadowed, worn by a dozen centuries. He recalls Quimby's statement: 'This is authentic.' And why the anthropologist had no doubt is clear enough.

Muhlbach lightly taps the Mayan with the jeweler's glass. The statuette responds with a hard dry note of ringing importance.

He puts both objects aside and sits for a long time with his hands folded beneath his chin. He contemplates the snow building up on the window ledge and hears the sizzle of logs in the fireplace, and it seems to him that now he understands the difference between a creation and an imitation.

But then there's the Olmec. Strange how convincing it could be in one light, how false in another.

After a while he begins to read:

A powerful and gifted race appeared suddenly in Mexico during the middle of the Preclassic Period without leaving a trace of any earlier developmental stage. The origin of these people and their extraordinary culture is one of the most important of the various unresolved enigmas of American archaeology. Major centers have been excavated at Tres Zapotes, Cerro de las Mesas and San Lorenzo. But the most significant of these temple cities must have been at La Venta, whose beginnings go back as far as 1000 B.C. Here on an island surrounded by pestilential mangrove swamps the Olmecs built plazas, colonnaded courts, pyramid-shaped platforms, carved altars, and raised monumental stone slabs covered with bas-relief sculpture of the highest artistic excellence.

They knew how to handle the hardest stones, particularly jade, with unequaled skill, and imposed their forms upon it with the certainty of perfected technique. No evolutionary steps have been found; their art seems to have flowered full-blown. The jades show a deceptive refinement coupled with great simplicity—the sensuously modeled and polished surfaces often incised with characteristic sharpness. These lines serve to illuminate details of the figures or objects, and frequently depict stylized Olmec profiles that appear again and again as decorative and probably magic elements. Unlike the lapidaries of succeeding cultures whose forms and style were limited by the hardness of stone and by the mechanical methods employed, the Olmecs completely dominated their materials. They employed all the processes known to later times: cutting the stone with a string, abrasion, crumbling by percussion, drilling with bone and stone drills, and polishing with finely powdered hard materials. Their jades have the same strong flowing forms that are found in their clay figures. In fact, regardless of the substance used, the distinctive Olmec style cannot be mistaken.

Very close to the famous La Venta jaguar god mosaic an offertorial cache of ax-shaped celts and superb jade and serpentine figures was discovered— fifteen jade figures standing in a semi-circle facing a single serpentine figure, with the flat jade celts forming a palisade. The meaning of this cache and the ritual it portrays has not been determined. The figurines, each of which is about eight inches in height, all show men standing in a typical Olmec stance, with flexed legs and loosely hanging arms, the head thrown slightly back, a position which brings to mind the stance of dancers as well as a state of religious trance. They represent the Olmec physical type of relatively short, squat fleshy men with clean-shaven, elongated, almost pear-shaped heads, a deformation effected by binding the head in infancy. Their short noses have perforations in the septum indicating the wearing of nose ornaments. Other typical Olmec traits showing in these figurines are fleshy necks, heavy jowls, stubborn chins and decidedly Mongoloid eyes with puffed eyelids. The most important characteristic, however, is the mouth—drawn down at the corners like that of a crying baby, and often emphasizing a thick flaring lip that suggests the fierce mouth of a jaguar. Since the jaguar was the great deity of the Olmecs, they felt a deep mystical affinity with this powerful king of the jungle, and to him they dedicated their splendid art and ritual.

The masks and figures so far uncovered seem to represent two distinct variations of the Olmec physical type. One had a broad flat nose and heavy lips, similar to the colossal basalt heads, although the crying-baby or jaguar aspect is more heavily emphasized. The other type is notable for a high-bridge aquiline nose and relatively thin lips. The two types are easily recognized, but their implication is one of the many fascinating aspects of Olmec culture that await full exploration and study.

So much has yet to be learned about these people who, by means of meticulous observations carried on through the centuries, apparently devised the first calendar in the New World and originated a manner of calendric notation that produced the earliest forms of glyph writing. These crucial inventions were only part of the legacy left by the Olmecs—a legacy heavily drawn upon by the Maya and their contemporaries all across Middle America.

Where did these people come from? What might be the significance of a curious similarity to the early Chavin culture of Peru, or to a haunting Oriental feeling evident in so many Olmec artifacts? In Mexico the name *chalchihuitl* and the glyphs for jade were synonyms of 'jewel' or 'precious'; in China the character *Yü* that stands for jade also means 'jewel' or 'treasure.' Furthermore, is it mere coincidence that both Chinese and Mexicans painted their funeral jades with bright red cinnabar?

Principally because the most archaic Olmec forms have been excavated in Guerrero and Oaxaca, Covarrubias believes that the origins of Olmec culture may one day be found along the coast and in the valleys of these two Pacific states, implying some remote connection with the Orient.

Bushnell believes the tropical Gulf Coast lowlands of southern Veracruz and Tabasco to have been its cradle, a view seemingly supported by Hasso von Winning who points to the occurrence of unmistakable Olmec traits beyond the heartland of Veracruz —at Tlatilco, Morelos, and to the southeast as far as San Salvador—as evidence of the vigor with which the Olmecs disseminated their ideals.

Alexander von Wuthenau subscribes to the migrant theory, although he feels that it remains an open question whether these people arrived in the New World via the Bering Strait or by trans-Pacific contact.

Jiménez Moreno suggests that the proto-Olmecs, peoples of Totonac-Zoquean stock who came from the south, probably from the Pacific coasts of Chiapas and Guatemala, drifted up the Isthmus of Tehuantepec to the Veracruz littoral.

Yet all authorities, though they disagree on the origins and migrations, seem to be in accord that no higher sculptural expression than that produced by the Olmecs has been discovered on the American continent.

Muhlbach puts the book aside. He sits motionless, his fingers forming a steeple just beyond the tip of his nose, and considers the import of what he has read. For one thing, should the mask turn out to be authentic it would be worth a fortune.

This happy possibility, however remote, begins to shine with somewhat less brilliance when he reads an article in the Sunday paper. All over the world, it seems, important works of art, both ancient and modern, are being stolen. Not too many years ago this happened so seldom that it was regarded as little more than a nuisance. Now, because of the prices being paid for first-rate works, it has become an international plague. Sometimes the thieves demand ransom, at other times the object simply vanishes into a private collection. Or it may go into a bank vault until the statute of limitations on stolen goods has expired. Or, if the thief becomes alarmed, it may be destroyed.

Stolen masterpieces catalogued by Interpol would furnish a museum. Within the past ten years more than a thousand major paintings and works of sculpture have disappeared, their total value conservatively estimated at one hundred million dollars. Paintings by Masaccio, Lautrec, Memling, Correggio,

Hals, Velázquez, Gainsborough. Sculpture by Praxiteles, Agesander, Phidias—the list goes on and on.

Thieves are also plundering archaeological sites. In fact, say some authorities, every known archaeological complex, if left unguarded, will have been robbed by the end of the present century. According to Dr. Enamul Haque of the Dacca museum, for example, during the past few years many Hindu temples have been looted—thousands of pieces of sculpture sawed or hacked from the walls and pedestals. Dr. Haque believes that much of this medieval artwork, probably most of it, already has been smuggled abroad for sale to private collectors.

Pakistan. Egypt. Burma. Cambodia. Nepal. Iraq. Everywhere the story is the same. But nowhere can the process of despoliation be observed half so clearly as in Central and South America.

Thirty years ago a market for Nazca ceramics or Mayan stelae did not exist. Carved limestone tablets or fantastically painted pots from the eighth century were called 'specimens' and could be bought for a few dollars. Now they are looked upon as masterpieces of color and design and are priced in the thousands. The consequence of this aesthetic reappraisal has been a ferocious assault on what little is left of early American civilizations. Looters using light planes, helicopters, diamond-tipped power tools, polyester casts and other technological innovations are stripping ancient ruins of everything which might conceivably have market value.

In the Mexican states of Campeche, Tabasco, Chiapas and Quintana Roo, as well as in the steamy Petén jungle of Guatemala, hundreds of tombs and temples, some of which pre-date Christianity, have been devastated by *estileros* and *huaqueros* seeking artifacts to satisfy the demand of wealthy collectors. At Piedras Negras on the Usumacinta River, for instance, the most important stelae have disappeared. Jimbal. Naranjo. Yaxha. Uolantum. Dos Pilas. El Zapote. El Caribe. La Florida. All of these sites have been raided, the chronology of generations blasted and flung aside.

In southern Campeche an entire stucco panel was removed under the supervision of an art dealer from the United States. Eight feet high and thirty feet in width, it was sawed into chunks, crated, shipped to New York and offered to the Metropolitan Museum for half a million dollars. Fortunately this panel was returned to Mexico where it may now be seen at the National Museum of Anthropology, but for every such work of art that is intercepted and repatriated countless others are successfully exported and sold, either to museums which all too often avoid asking questions, or to individual collectors who seldom concern themselves with ethical problems.

Naturally the theft of monumental items such as the Campeche panel is what most disturbs government authorities, but the loss of small objects is also serious because things stolen from prehistoric graves and ceremonial centers are difficult to correlate. The mask, effigy, knife or dish becomes an orphan, provocative by itself, but able to tell the archaeologist only a fraction of what he might otherwise deduce. Out of context, however attractive it may be mounted on a pedestal, it is less than it was. And thousands of pre-Columbian bowls, carved jades, gold ornaments and terra cotta figurines are now for sale in galleries throughout Europe and America.

Muhlbach, folding his Sunday paper, drops it to the floor. He sits for a long time looking thoughtfully at the Mayan magistrate.

The Mayan is a fait accompli—far from home, for better or worse. Too late to ask how or when he was abducted. Nor is it likely that the mask could be returned, even if Piglett were willing to talk. The mask must have gone through a good many hands, each palm crossed with enough silver to guarantee silence. So, granted the best of intentions, who could discover the original site? This is not my fault, he thinks. In neither case am I to blame.

Nevertheless, there's a difference between a small clay piece and an important jade. The Mayan is splendid. Excellent. But the mask—if it's real I have no right to own that. Assuming it's what I suspect it is, that thing belongs in Mexico in the National Museum of Anthropology. And in a few days I should know for certain. God help me if I picked up a national treasure.

With great difficulty he prevents himself from calling the museum on Monday to find out if Sanchez has returned, if he has had a chance to study the mask, and what his opinion might be. By Tuesday the man must have had time enough. More than enough.

Steeped in anxiety Muhlbach begins to wonder if it will be possible to live through the week.

Friday, having been delayed by a series of unexpected clients toward whom he barely contrived to remain civil, he arrives at the museum much later than he had planned and rides the elevator to the fifth floor with gradually increasing apprehension.

The hall is empty. Sanchez's door, of course, is locked. He had known it would be locked. All the way across town he had been absolutely sure Sanchez would be gone.

The white-haired gentleman, just as inevitably, is at the rolltop desk reading a magazine. As soon as he glances up a shadow of dismay crosses his distinguished face. He drops the magazine, goes to the table and starts moving papers around, looking underneath the mimeographed bulletins and pamphlets and large Manila envelopes and correspondence, pausing occasionally to frown or tap his forehead.

And finally there it is.

Knew it had to be here! Doggone, I completely forgot about this. Meant to give it to Paco the first of the week. Had lunch with him on Monday, as a matter of fact. I suppose all I can do is apologize.

By the indifference with which he handles the mask Muhlbach can see that he considers it worthless. Of course he may be unfamiliar with pre-Columbian art. His specialty could be Eskimo or African or Oceanic. He might even be an administrator instead of an anthropologist, in which case his opinion wouldn't mean anything. But still, he knows. He knows. The look in his eye—his attitude—something or other indicates that he knows all about the mask.

You especially wanted Sanchez to see this, did you?

The question could be interpreted a couple of ways. However, the emphasis seems to have fallen not so much on the idea of somebody examining the mask as it has on the name of Sanchez.

Not necessarily. I was told at the desk that Mr. Sanchez would examine it. The fact is, I was rather hopeful that Dr. Ekholm might be able to give me an opinion.

At this the white-haired gentleman peers across the top of his glasses, fixing Muhlbach for a long moment with an indecipherable gaze.

Ekholm, you say?

Dr. Ekholm was busy, according to the receptionist.

I see. I see.

After another interminable moment he continues:

Since we've missed Sanchez, suppose I have a look at it. Will that do?

That would be fine.

Then suppose you take a chair, Mr. Muhlbach, while I just study this fellow.

Muhlbach draws a chair up close to the desk,

seats himself and leans forward in order not to miss anything.

Not much happens. After having turned it over several times, fingered it and gazed at it with benevolent apathy, the old gentleman makes a clucking noise. Then he clears his throat.

I might just find out what the microscope can tell us.

Certainly. Do whatever you need to do. Any information you could give me would be appreciated.

Very good, sir. Help yourself to a magazine. I'll be back presently.

He gets up and walks out of the room, limping slightly, carrying the Olmec with no more respect than he would carry a paperweight.

Muhlbach crosses his legs, folds his arms and looks around. There's very little to see. Nothing unusual. More or less what one would expect in a museum office. A filing cabinet not quite closed. Books. Stacks of paper. An apple. A family photograph in a leatherette frame. A Swiss calendar—one of those gingerbread Alpine chalets in a meadow of impossibly brilliant flowers. At the same time, though, the barren cubicle is rather satisfying. A person could sit here hour after hour without being distracted. It would be a good place to read and to think. And whoever this gentleman is, he must be a member of the anthropology staff, because all those technical pamphlets and ethnological books wouldn't belong to an administrator.

At the sound of footsteps echoing along the corridor he straightens up to compose himself for the news. The examination hasn't taken very long, not as long as it should.

The news is brief. At both corners of the mouth and inside both nostrils the microscope has revealed striations caused by a power drill.

Well then, Muhlbach replies after a deep breath, I guess that settles the business.

Oh, I shouldn't call it final. Now and again we come upon miniature jade bottles made by the Olmecs which have been worked over with metal tools. Peasants find them, and because they know tourists prefer shiny things they take these bottles to friend José who works in the garage and knows how to use a drill. He puts a nice finish on them and drills a hole through the solid end so they can be strung together to make an attractive necklace of beads. The striations on this mask, therefore, don't prove that your mask is a fake. But what we can be pretty sure of is that an automatic tool was used on it.

You seem to be suggesting that this could be a legitimate Olmec mask which was polished up for the tourist trade.

No. I shouldn't think it likely.

May I ask why not?

We must take several matters into consideration. This reddish stain would seem to be an attempt to imitate the traces of iron oxide we sometimes find on Olmec jades, but it can be quite readily wiped off with a little acetone. Then there's the matter of the edges, the absence of surface disintegration, the sculptural quality, certain details of the carving which aren't quite right, and a number of other things. In a nutshell, I'm afraid I should say this was made not long ago. Not very long ago.

Would you say it was made in Guerrero?

I wouldn't care to speculate.

Muhlbach picks up his discovery, which now feels cold and unpleasant. The man must think I'm an idiot, he says to himself. Well, I should have known. Not one dealer made a bid on the mask.

I bought it at an auction, he remarks, although he had not intended to say this. The words seem to expand like balloons and gently sink toward the floor with excruciating prominence.

Not often will you find authentic pieces on a bargain table, Mr. Muhlbach. No, not often. A mask as important as this—if indeed it were an old one—oh, that would be international news. A goodly number of people—oh, men with quite a lot of experience—have spent a lifetime searching for just such items with no success whatever. Which means it's unlikely, you see.

I can understand that.

I've not brought you a good report, I'm afraid.

Certainly it could have been better. But I appreciate what you've told me, nevertheless. And I want to thank you for your time.

Not at all, sir. You're most welcome. Sorry about that Sanchez business.

Muhlbach, getting to his feet, replies that Sanchez could not have been more instructive. He picks up the mask and makes an effort to smile.

Thank you again.

Yes, yes. Goodby. Don't feel badly. The money—oh, that's another matter. But you mustn't worry about having been tricked. Most of us are tricked sooner or later. The point is, you see, to hold it to a minimum.

Well, there's no longer any sense arguing that the mask could be genuine. After two appraisals—or three, including the mysterious Maureen—it's time to admit the truth. I did persuade myself, he thinks while waiting for the elevator. I wanted so much to believe. I like to pretend I'm incapable of self-deceit, but I'm as gullible as anybody else.

With hands clasped behind his back he waits, eyes fixed on the hair ribbon of a schoolgirl, and finds himself wondering if he should show the mask to at least one other authority. After all, Guy and the museum anthropologist both might be mistaken.

But then the elevator door slides open, he steps in, and as the door rolls smoothly shut he shakes his head against that last desperate hope. If one has been swindled one might as well face the fact.

No, he thinks, that isn't quite how it was. Piglett represented the mask as Mexican, nothing else. I was the connoisseur who labeled it Olmec. All right, I gypped myself. My 'intuitive' knowledge. Absurd. What a conceit. I should have known better. Maureen said it in a word: Experience. But great God that was an expensive lesson, almost a hundred dollars. And the embarrassment. Guy thinks I'm a jackass, so does she. And the old gentleman upstairs. Yes, and so does Piglett, naturally. And probably Holmgren. Lord, Lord! And that Dominick fellow—he looked at me while I was standing in line to pay for it. Half the people at the auction must have realized it was fake. What a spectacle I made of myself.

The elevator stops. The door trundles open and he walks rapidly toward the exit. It will be good to rejoin a commonplace world which knows little and cares even less about such esoteric topics as Olmec sculpture.

Outside the museum a dry hard snow rides diagonally up the street. The temperature has dropped. Squinting through the snow which beats at him like soap flakes Muhlbach begins to pull on his gloves. At that moment somebody bumps against him.

He turns around to find a girl in a ski sweater with an armload of books. Her hair is blowing across her face, which perhaps explains why she was unable to see where she was going. Something about her seems familiar. Then he recognizes the harried expression.

Ah ha! Did you ever locate Miss Pellegrini?

After staring at him with a look of wild mistrust the girl claps one hand to her lips.

Oh! Last Friday. No. Miss Pellegrini had left for the weekend.

I see. Well, I'm not surprised. Did she go to Vermont?

Vermont?

Did she by any chance spend the weekend in Vermont?

How should I know? God, I was only trying to find her. It was hideous. Oh!—the bus! Goodby!

Muhlbach watches her run toward the bus, waving and calling. She's mad, he thinks, hopelessly mad. Just then a gust of wind almost takes his hat off. He settles it more firmly and continues down the steps with the mask bumping against his thigh.

He decides to walk a few blocks. It may take some time to adjust to the disappointment and a little fresh air might help.

While walking he discusses the situation with himself. It's not the least bit pleasant to admit you've been a fool. A priceless jade mask at a fourth-rate auction. Lord, what got into me? A child should know better. Strange, we can be quite aware of something but then conveniently forget it. Well, psychologists claim we're able to believe anything we wish to believe. I must say I won't doubt that from now on.

The snow drops straight down with threatening insistence, stops for a few minutes and then swirls in lazy cross currents while Muhlbach marches through Columbus Circle reflecting on the past couple of months. So many fresh perceptions have developed from such an insignificant seed—perceptions which could have flowered years ago, or never, depending on some accidental circumstance. How odd. And what will happen next?

Where am I taking myself? he wonders. Or do I delude myself once again by assuming that I control the direction of my life? Why is it that nothing except pre-Columbian art seems to matter much anymore? That's an exaggeration, of course. Otto and Donna, for instance, mean more than all the world's Olmec masks. But still, it's true. These artifacts have become precious, though I can't explain why they should seem valuable to me now when they seemed valueless before I visited Taos. Yet they do. I'm obsessed by them. I can't understand it.

He remembers that when Balzac was dying he insisted somebody send for Dr. Bianchon because Bianchon could save him. Bianchon, the fictitious Bianchon, a doctor who existed only in the mind of Balzac.

So that's it, Muhlbach thinks. I can't distinguish reality any longer. I'm gripped by an obsession. I suppose I should be alarmed, but as a matter of fact I'm not. This is really rather pleasant. I want more. Do all deluded persons feel the same? Do they all plead for more? And if they do, how does it end?

He realizes that he has walked almost to Times Square.

He steps into a doorway to get out of the wind for a few moments and to look around, because he has not been walking idly but with deep determination, as though he knew where he was going. His hands are cold. His feet are cold. The afternoon light has begun to fade. I'm slightly batty, he thinks. What am I doing here?

Then he understands that he has been walking toward the Village. But why? Well, to visit Arthur Guy—either to talk with him or to have a look at his merchandise. To address him as Dr. Bianchon, perhaps, though the connection isn't quite clear. In any case, there's no sense walking the entire distance.

He stands in the doorway, which is somewhat warmer than the street, clapping his hands and stamping his feet, rushing toward the curb with one finger lifted whenever a taxi approaches.

At last one stops behind a shower of slush.

THE gallery is just off Washington Square on the first floor of a brownstone. Alongside the stoop a wooden sign swings in the wind.

BONAMPAK

Bonampak. An ancient Mayan city. He remembers that the word means 'painted walls.'

He climbs the steps and tries the doorknob. Nothing happens. However, not many doors are left unlocked these days. He presses the button and is answered by a familiar electrical buzz.

Bonampak turns out to be one long narrow whitewashed room with a high ceiling. Two sinister tropical plants which undoubtedly eat small animals and children are guarding the entrance, everything else is pre-Columbian. Terra cotta figures, stone carvings, a stucco head, remnants of prehistoric textiles, pots, beads, gold jewelry.

In a swivel chair behind the desk sits Maureen, costumed as a sailor in bell-bottom dungarees and a jumper with a striped red bib. She is smoking a cigarillo and it occurs to Muhlbach that she resembles a magazine illustration.

He wanders toward her, pulling off his gloves, not certain if she has recognized him. She may be nearsighted.

Arthur? she inquires, lifting her voice.

Guy answers from directly overhead: Que pasa? You owe me a buck.

Muhlbach hears footsteps descending. A door creaks. Guy enters. In his yellow turtleneck sweater and skintight brown corduroys he looks every bit as fashionable as his lady.

Hello hello hello! he exclaims, shaking hands. Good to see you. Make yourself at home. Coffee's about to boil, I'll be down in a minute.

He goes back upstairs.

Maureen waves at a chair with her cigarillo, but Muhlbach decides to investigate the gallery instead of sitting down.

I gather you've been expecting me.

He wasn't. I was. Did you take your mask to the museum?

I've just come from there.

What did they tell you?

Essentially what you told me.

There wasn't much doubt.

Did you and Mr. Guy study the mask before the auction?

We glanced at it. The thing was a patent fraud.

That obvious?

A better imitation might be found at Gimbels. I'm sorry you lacked the expertise to recognize it.

You sound quite knowledgeable.

I regard myself as an educated amateur.

Would it be impertinent to ask how you 'educated' yourself?

I lived for some time in Mérida. Naturally I visited Chichén. Then Uxmal and Labná and Sayil. It grew on me. It does, you know.

So I've been told.

She laughs. That's why I bet on you. Arthur thought you'd be too embarrassed about the mask to come back, but I said no—he'll be around. I suggest you look at your misfortune this way, Mr. Muhlbach. No interior decorator would sell you a jadeite mask of that size for the price you paid.

Interior decorating does not interest me.

I sympathize. However, you should bear in mind that you are not the first person to buy a fake.

Muhlbach, strolling around the gallery, considers this. What she has said may be a trifle pious, but at the same time it does soothe the burn. Not much, but a little. In any event the mask is a dead issue. Talking about it is disagreeable.

I'm surprised to find Bonampak in the Village. Wouldn't you do better uptown?

It would be different. Arthur would feel enslaved by the rent. Here we have some freedom.

She points to the Jalisco couple on a shelf.

We paid a lot for that, as you know. We've priced it very reasonably. Norris Dominick would be forced to ask a great deal more.

Muhlbach walks across to look at the Jalisco. Whimsically attached to the rump of the female is a round white sticker marked eight hundred dollars.

Next to the couple is a Veracruz smiling face mounted on a polished walnut pedestal: three hundred and fifty dollars.

Beside the Veracruz stands a bowlegged cowboy from Colima: ninety-five.

Next to the cowboy sits a pensive little man with his chin resting on one knee. The back of his heart-shaped head is disintegrating and he has been broken into as many fragments as Humpty Dumpty and glued together again. The sticker on his neck says twelve hundred.

Chinesco, Maureen remarks. An unusually good one.

I must admit I find pre-Columbian prices somewhat startling.

Have you visited any other galleries?

No, and if this is an indication I don't believe I could stand it.

You'd be more than somewhat startled. Beginning

collectors invariably are shocked to realize what it can cost. But in building a collection, Mr. Muhlbach, the familiar truth applies that you get what you pay for. Some collectors may be satisfied with common pieces, others demand the best. It's up to you.

In other words, Muhlbach says to himself, I ought to declare my intentions. Do I plan to spend only a few dollars or do I want the best? Of course that's why he pays her—because I assume she works for him. They've got to sell this stuff. Nevertheless, it annoys me. I don't need hints.

How is the gallery doing?

Are we successful? Very. More and more people are becoming pre-Columbian enthusiasts. Though Arthur has never been obliged to depend on gallery sales.

After thinking about this Muhlbach shakes his head. I don't understand.

Oh, she replies, blowing a plume of smoke, I thought you knew. Guy, Dietzel and Craig.

And who might they be?

It is an advertising agency, Mr. Muhlbach.

I see.

Most people know of it.

Ah. Well, at any rate, Mr. Guy's principal source of income would be from the agency, making Bonampak more or less a hobby. Would that be right?

Not in the least. Arthur seldom goes to the office. He had a direct line installed which enables him to conduct agency affairs from here. It works out splendidly.

What do Dietzel and Craig say about this arrangement?

The accounts haven't suffered. What else matters?

The situation sounds ideal.

Idyllic, really.

Now why couldn't I do that? he wonders. Why

not make some changes in my life? God knows I'm sick of the routine. My life's already half gone, why use the last half like the first? Why not live as I'd like to?

Improbable schemes come flickering into view with the ephemeral brilliance of butterflies:

Borrow enough money to buy a percentage of Bonampak.

Move a desk into the gallery and open a line to the office.

Put on a turtleneck sweater and obscene trousers and hunt for a beautiful girl. Maybe Maureen has a sister.

He picks up a small chipped flint, pretending to examine it. Maureen observes him through narrowed eyes.

That comes from Campeche, probably eighth or ninth century. It was discovered at the base of a dated stela, according to our source. A few years from now you won't be able to buy those at any price, much less what Arthur is asking. I've told him it's ridiculous, but he says we got it for very little so we can sell it for very little.

Muhlbach puts down the flint.

We also have a large obsidian ceremonial object from the same area, which is in the safe. I'd be glad to get it out.

Not at the moment, thank you.

Maureen inspects the ash of her cigarillo. Closing a deal might be the last thing on her mind. That cameo profile hides a saleswoman as tough as a logger's boot.

Tell me, do Mr. Guy's partners share his pre-Columbian enthusiasm?

Hardly. They're convinced Arthur is mad. Pre-Columbian bores them sick. One of them plays golf at every conceivable opportunity and the other devotes himself to screwing chorus girls. What about you, Mr. Muhlbach? What do you do?

Insurance. Metropolitan Mutual.

Arthur guessed Standard Oil or General Motors. I said no, the caste marks are different.

Have I been insulted?

Maureen smiles, leaning back in the swivel chair. Oh, not really. There's hope for you. Then she raises her voice: Arthur?

He answers distinctly: Sí, querida! Yo me voy pronto. Tenemos hormigas.

Honestly, she mutters. Those ants. We've tried everything.

She reaches into a desk drawer, but instead of ant powder she brings out a small stone carving of a man with crossed arms.

Good or bad, Mr. Muhlbach?

Am I supposed to authenticate this?

She doesn't answer, but continues holding it up for inspection.

All right, let's have a look.

She offers him a jeweler's glass somewhat larger than his own. The magnification seems to be about the same, although it covers a wider field.

While he is examining the surface Guy walks in awkwardly carrying three cups of coffee.

Your friend Varda was here a couple of hours ago. Too bad you missed him.

As usual, Maureen adds, he accused us of being thieves. We're lucky if he doesn't call us anything worse. 'Hell, you ought to be locked up!' she exclaims with a scowl. 'God damn it, I could buy this for twenty pesos in Morelia. Jesus Christ, they got better stuff in the flea market!' Really, Arthur, you should have a talk with him. When other people are in the gallery it's humiliating.

Claude likes to make noise.

I'm sure Mrs. Lowenfeld wouldn't stand for such vulgarity.

Guy shrugs. He looks at the carving. I see you got our problem child.

Does that mean you aren't sure of it?

Tell me what you think. Then I'll give you the rundown.

Well, Muhlbach reflects, considering that I've got a fake Olmec as big as a tombstone in my pocket this is very flattering. They're having fun with me, but that's all right.

After a sip of coffee he resumes studying the figure. Stylistically there can be no doubt that it's Mezcala with traces of Chontal influence. The naturalistic stance, for one thing, and the earplugs. Arms crossed on the breast—yes, that rather touching acknowledgement of life would be Chontal. Not quite so rigid and architectonic. The feet are curious, stubbier than most. Bisected eyebrows, an unusual feature. Even so, it looks good. On the whole, yes, it does look right. The size might be questionable— perhaps too large. Larger than those illustrated in the books, at any rate. Yet it seems to have an authentic Guerrero quality.

He tries to recall if there might have been a figure like this in the museum. Olmecs were to the right just inside the entrance. Remojadas farther back. Mayan pottery along the south wall. West Coast to the left, not far from the entrance—those massive Jaliscos, Nayarits and so forth—but what about Guerrero?

Well?

Tentatively I say yes. But let me have another moment.

Take as much time as you need. He's tough.

The stone is dark green, it might very well be porphyry. Nothing wrong with that. The edges, however, feel fresh. Yet in dry soil a stone would scarcely be affected by the centuries, so how do you decide?

Again he peers at it through the jeweler's glass.

Finally he puts down the glass and hands the statue to Maureen.

Here's my opinion. From the style I thought it was good but now I've got some doubts. I'll say that in my judgment it's recent. On the other hand, because you have it here in the gallery I'd say it must be authentic.

Mr. Muhlbach, have you considered entering politics?

Or law? Guy asks. I mean, that was beautiful.

Thank you. Now tell me, is the piece old?

After popping his knuckles and flicking an invisible speck of lint from his sweater Guy admits that he can't make up his mind.

Maureen runs her fingertips across the surface.

It isn't here. It is not here. I simply do not get stone against stone.

Would you explain that?

An old piece would have been cut with stone tools, Mr. Muhlbach, and polished by hand with natural abrasives. Counterfeiters seldom go to so much trouble.

Well, he thinks, I tried that stunt myself at the auction and got burned. Maybe her fingers are more sensitive but I wouldn't bet on it. She ridiculed me for trying to feel my way into the mask, now she's doing the same thing. I don't understand these pre-Columbian people.

The source is good, Mo. We haven't gotten a single bad piece from Max. You remember that rattlesnake? Everybody turned thumbs down, but then Carlos okayed it. If this one's bad it'll be the first. It scares me. I admit it scares me, but I got a feeling it's good.

What a peculiar business, Muhlbach thinks.

Mr. Guy, you told me that in questionable cases you went to the museum.

Yep. And they kept this little joker a month. They don't trust him but they can't prove anything's wrong.

No mechanical striations?

Not a damn thing.

Stone is impossible, Mr. Muhlbach. Practically all of it is fake. You've got to be so cautious. Stone and gold. Gold is an absolute horror.

If the museum is either unable or unwilling to authenticate this figure, what do you do?

Get more opinions. A museum verdict isn't the final answer. I know for a fact some pieces they said were bad were perfectly okay, and vice versa. Norris had a beautiful diorite eagle three or four years ago that he felt was just too good to be real. The museum said it was okay. Then later Norris met the guy who carved it. So we get more opinions. Carlos Ruiz, for one. He's on a dig in British Honduras but he'll be back next month.

If Carlos likes it, Arthur, I don't think you should have any hesitation.

Is the piece for sale?

Not on your life. That's why it's in the drawer. We've got to feel certain.

Suppose your Carlos Ruiz turns out to be as skeptical as the museum?

Don't know. Depends. If he's pretty negative I may hand it over to a decorator and swallow the loss.

Let me ask a question which may be offensive. Considering that you obtained this item from a reliable source, and taking into account the fact that the museum was unable to find anything specifically wrong, why don't you offer it as an authentic pre-Columbian piece?

Guy, as usual, is less articulate than Maureen.

Because, Mr. Muhlbach, the castle would come tumbling down. Quite apart from the ethical issue, there is the matter of economics. If word gets around that a dealer is selling dubious pieces he will very soon begin to lose customers. No intelligent dealer would take such a risk. Does that answer your question?

Yes. But I have another.

Heaven help us.

Muhlbach turns to Guy. You once mentioned a ceremonial ax from Guatemala which you had gone over, as I recall, 'a hundred times.' Furthermore, you said that everybody who looked at it had a different opinion.

Right.

Have you sold it?

We gave it to Mo's nephew.

For his twelfth birthday, she adds. He just loves it.

But you never knew for certain whether or not it was authentic?

Nope.

Well, Muhlbach reflects, this business confounds me. Nothing about it makes sense. I absolutely do not understand how these people operate.

Maureen opens a bottom drawer of the desk and takes out one of the famous barking dogs.

Another problem?

That's for you to decide.

He picks up the dog and the jeweler's glass.

The body is mottled with hundreds of black blotches, some so small that even under the lens they can hardly be seen. If the piece was buried these blotches should be manganese dioxide, either inherent to the clay or leached from the soil. Or they could be microscopic cities of bacteria. The question is whether or not these discolorations actually came about through centuries of burial or whether they are skillful imitations. I don't know enough, he thinks. I've learned just enough to be irritated by my ignorance.

He studies the paint, which resembles the mud of a prehistoric lake bed. Would half an hour in the oven turn factory fresh paint into old paint?

One of the paws has been broken, however the break doesn't look recent. No sharp edge. But of course it might have been sandpapered.

What else? Dozens of nicks and scratches, some relatively new, others that seem to have weathered a good many years. The teeth and nostrils are caked with grit, which may or may not mean much. Anything else? Signs of erosion? Nothing definite. Pressure cracks? None visible. Wait—yes, a long faint crack along the haunch. But is it the result of age or of clumsy manufacturing?

Then on the underside of the muzzle he discovers a root trace. Ah ha! This proves the dog was buried.

What have you decided?

It's good.

Why?

He summarizes what he has found, adding that in terms of style there doesn't seem to be anything wrong. The dog very closely resembles one of the dogs in the national museum in Mexico City—at least according to a photograph. But principally because of the root trace. The root trace was convincing.

Excellent! says Maureen. You're showing great progress. However, this happens to be a fake. The black splotches are nothing more than black paint spattered on with a toothbrush. The grit packed around the teeth is a mixture of glue and dirt. The paw was broken deliberately.

They don't like to damage the face, Guy continues. Fakers will snap off tails and ears and legs. In fact they'll break a piece in half, even though it lowers the market value, but they won't damage a face. Maybe chip the muzzle, but nothing serious. And they almost never touch the eyes.

Which is especially true in the case of human effigies, Maureen goes on. A lip, a nose, an ear, a chin, yes. But they simply cannot bring themselves to blind the figures. Isn't that fascinating? And your 'root trace,' Mr. Muhlbach, was created by pressing a length of thread into the wet clay. Although at times we do see genuine root traces which have been artificially induced. A piece may be wrapped in damp cloth with some bean sprouts, for instance, so that in a matter of weeks you will have more roots than you can count.

Guy turns the statue upside down and draws a circle around a small area of the belly.

Put your glass on that. Tell me what you find.

Muhlbach inspects everything within the circle. Nothing unusual. A few of the imitation manganese dioxide spots, a few scratches.

Look. Guy begins drawing on the back of an envelope. He elongates several of the spots so that they resemble teardrops.

Muhlbach peers through the glass again. Yes. There they are. And the teardrops all are falling in the same direction.

Sometimes the paint will run. The fakers are careful because it's a dead giveaway, but once in a while it happens—usually on a curved surface.

Would this be one of Ignacio's masterpieces?

Nacio likes to work in stone, Guy remarks while frowning at the dog. I'm not sure who made this. I got it in a village near Manzanillo on my last trip.

Why did you want a fake?

Maureen laughs.

What it comes down to is that he thought the dog was genuine. There was no electricity in the village and he had to inspect it by flashlight. It did feel heavy, as though the clay might still be full of water, even so he thought it was good.

Maureen pulls another fraud from the desk, a miniature brownstone Teotihuacán mask the size of a walnut. She explains that both the size and the shape are wrong. The features are wrong. Look at the mouth. That mouth could not possibly have been carved in the fifth or sixth century.

Why not?

None of us can escape from the twentieth century, Mr. Muhlbach. Our attitudes in regard to everything—politics, religion, food, entertainment, art—are conditioned by the circumstances of the age. In the same way Fragonard was conditioned by the eighteenth century. Giotto was conditioned by the fourteenth. You understand what I'm saying, certainly.

Not altogether.

Then let us take Chagall, who is so much a product of the twentieth century. Now let us project ourselves several centuries into the future and say we are confronted by a 'Chagall.' Is it a genuine Chagall or a twenty-fourth-century imitation? If it is a fake— a twenty-fourth-century fake—our sensibilities will tell us the truth. Assuming, of course, that we are thoroughly acquainted with the work of Chagall. Now you may ask why this is so. Because every forger, though he may be doing his best to duplicate the art of a certain period, will unconsciously reveal certain characteristics of his own time. In the same way, assuming we are intimately familiar with a given period of pre-Columbian art, we can detect the presence or absence of the characteristics of those times. Do you understand?

I'm not sure. Theoretically, perhaps. But in actual fact there must be a good many fakes on the market and in the museums which are considered authentic.

Oh, thousands! she answers with a lift of the eyebrows.

Well, there it is again, Muhlbach thinks. Lord, this business would drive me mad.

Let me show you a thing or two, says Guy. Look. The mask is soapstone, which you can almost scratch with your fingernail. That means it would be in pretty poor shape after fifteen centuries, yet this is in perfect condition. Now look here on the back. See the crude drilling? Whoever drilled this could do neat work, as you can see from the front. But on the back side, where it wouldn't detract from the face, he tried to suggest primitive workmanship.

Don't you think it has charm? Maureen asks. The conniving peasant who claimed to have excavated it was demanding a thousand pesos. Arthur eventually compromised on the price and gave him a dollar. I particularly like the juxtaposition of Teotihuacán features on an Olmec ellipse. They do that, you know—give a Mixtec lady a Nayarit nose ring, or invent a totally preposterous Tarascan helmet.

Guy walks to the shelf and returns with another barking dog. Both dogs are liberally speckled with black. Both are the same size and color. The only difference seems to be that the second one has a two hundred and fifty dollar tag.

Go over this carefully.

Muhlbach does so, then leans back to contemplate the animals side by side. But close up or from a distance they look identical. Nothing except the sticker distinguishes a two thousand year old pre-Columbian from the Manzanillo fake.

Now what? he asks himself. Truth and falsehood barking right in my face and if it weren't for that price tag I wouldn't know which was which.

He lifts both hands in a gesture of defeat.

Guy holds the expensive dog beneath the lamp.

Look here. Manganese is a metallic element. See how the light reflects?

Muhlbach lowers his head, squints, moves from side to side, and perceives what could be called a metallic blue reflection. It is extremely faint. He suspects it may be his imagination.

Paint won't produce that exact sheen. Notice, too, this three-dimensional quality. Manganese penetrates the clay instead of lying on the surface.

He leans forward with the glass next to one eye and his nose touching the dog's flank. Yes. Yes, the spots do show a certain roughness.

Look on the right side of the muzzle. Put the glass on that black snowflake or flower. That's a dendrite. So far they haven't come up with a method for imitating those.

Muhlbach studies the elegant branching structure, which is too dainty to be simulated with paint or ink.

Could they be reproduced chemically?

Not at present. Tomorrow, who knows? But up to now those dendrites say a lot. If the Mexicans were as patient as the Orientals we'd have more problems. Mexican fakes are seldom buried longer than ten or fifteen years and the soil can accomplish only so much during that time. Chinese fakes may be buried for a century or more. A man leaves them to his descendants the way we leave a trust fund.

Maureen suddenly inhales—that odd European mannerism which expresses agreement. Yes, it's true. A London dealer once showed me a calcified marble sword in late Chou style. Actually, it dated from the eighteenth century. Oh, but it was striking!

Have another look, Guy suggests, his fingers resting on the head of the pre-Columbian dog. You missed something pretty interesting. I'll give you a hint. The ears.

Muhlbach examines both ears from tip to base, but can find nothing remarkable.

Try again.

And now that Guy has insisted, now that he has all but pointed out the exact place, Muhlbach is able to discern what might be considered black weeds among the black flowers along the base of the left ear. Furthermore, those weeds are not manganese.

Guy explains that the ear was broken off, possibly while the statue was being excavated, and was glued back into position. Then a clay slip was added to conceal the break and this was spattered with black paint to give the impression of an undamaged piece.

Now why go to so much trouble? Maureen asks. Because the slightest break will affect market value. There are collectors who automatically refuse any piece that has been mended—though in this instance not many of them could detect the repair.

Yet you feel obligated to point it out?

Of course.

Might I ask why?

Two reasons. First, ethics. In common with most dealers we care about the gallery's reputation. The second reason is more prosaic. It's simply good business. The world of art is a small town bursting with gossip.

Guy brings another terra cotta down from the shelf. A Nayarit woman holding a child in her lap. This is a 'marriage.' The woman is authentic, the child has been faked.

Well, the problem of authenticity seems to be developing more branches than a dendrite. At any moment Guy will point to a couple of discolorations and announce that one is six months older than the other. But what difference does it make? Isn't aesthetic appreciation the main thing? Take that calcified sword. She was impressed by it even though it was an imitation. So if you are pleased with a sword or a painting or a Colima dog, why insist on authenticity?

Because we look at works of art just as we look at people in this respect: nobody likes a pretender.

Yes, all right. Granted. However, let's imagine a collector who buys a fake which he believes to be genuine. In other words, if I'm unable to tell the pre-Columbian dog from the imitation, aren't they equally good?

Objectively? Maureen asks. Yes. But remember that our perceptions are influenced by what we know. Take the Met's 'Etruscan' warrior. Don't we see him differently now than we did before the fraud was revealed? Or that bronze horse which was thought to be Greek but later was called a fake, and still later was restored to good standing. What we saw when we looked at that horse was not merely what our eyes recorded. Are we cameras, Mr. Muhlbach?

Well, that might be answered several ways, depending on one's viewpoint.

Let me propose a hypothetical situation. You are driving through the countryside. You see a distant hill simply alive with buttercups. How charming! How delightful it would be to wander through them. But when you arrive you find that instead of buttercups the hillside is littered with scraps of yellow paper. Now would it be the same? Surely not, and why? Because you have perceived the truth.

She puffs on her cigarillo.

Speaking of cameras reminds me. Once when I was a child I was shown a tintype of my great-grandmother and I was enchanted—utterly enchanted. Later we learned that the stern old lady wasn't great-grandmother. Who she was, in fact, nobody knew. From then on the tintype was only a curiosity.

Look, says Guy, you know the novelist Koestler?

He did an essay on this subject. He mentions being introduced to some woman at a cocktail party who ran a dressmaker's shop and who wanted to talk to him about his books, so he got away from her as fast as he could. Okay, a few minutes after that he's talking to somebody who asks what he thought of the princess. What princess? This woman who ran a dressmaker's shop—she also happened to be a princess. Koestler takes another look. Now she looks pretty darn fascinating.

Maureen picks up the story:

She had changed, you see, merely because Koestler's frame of reference had been enlarged. Everything about the woman assumed a different aspect. Even the lamentable fact that she had been reduced to such a petty bourgeois way of life struck him as significant. Even the dreadful banality of her conversation. But later that same evening he discovered that while she was indeed a princess, she was a princess by marriage. She was in fact a former mannequin, nothing else, and upon learning this he again found the poor creature frightfully dull. She could no longer stimulate his imagination, you see, because she was not an 'original.'

Guy continues:

Originals attract us for another reason, which goes all the way back to prehistoric belief in magical properties. If we own something original, whether it's a skull or a lock of hair or an autograph or a drawing, we think maybe we acquire a little of the strength or substance of whoever it belonged to or whoever made it.

As you can see, Mr. Muhlbach, the subject does grow involved.

It does, to say the least. Authenticity, subjectivity, morality, economics, aesthetics—I feel more comfortable dealing with insurance problems, he thinks while gazing at the lamp. In that world we do have our intangibles to sort out, our probabilities and our ethical considerations, but to no such degree as—now that lamp. That lamp. Why should I be staring at the lamp? Oh yes, the flashlight.

Tell me something, Mr. Guy. You said the village where you bought that fake dog had no electricity?

Right.

You spent the night there?

Yes. And I never met so many fleas.

Why didn't you examine the piece the next morning?

I left pretty early.

Before dawn?

I didn't want to talk to any *federales*.

Incredible, Muhlbach thinks. Absolutely incredible. This man will not sell an object of doubtful authenticity, yet he has no objection to smuggling.

Maureen interrupts. The situation has been changing, Mr. Muhlbach. Not only in Latin America but everywhere. Governments which had not cared in the slightest about their artistic heritage are now terribly possessive. Unreasonably so. Exporting pre-Columbian, for instance, has come to be regarded as a serious offense with jail sentences of up to nine years—which is ridiculous. Furthermore, the penalties are not levied equitably. Let me give you an example. We know a dealer who was fined three hundred thousand pesos for attempting to export a crate of Totonac material while customs agents at that same port of embarkation were actually guarding another dealer's shipment. So you see the picture is not altogether black and white.

It's more like Russian roulette, says Guy. He points to a locked display case. Have you seen that gold pectoral?

Arthur, my dear.

They exchange a look.

Well, whatever he was about to say isn't going to

be said. At least not now. One of her duties, apparently, is to keep the lid on her employer.

Muhlbach walks over to the case.

The pectoral is cast gold in the shape of a frog, unusually large, with inlaid turquoise disks.

A splendid piece, Mr. Muhlbach. You may recognize the style as Mixtec. Our guess is that it came from Yanhuitlán.

Mixtec it may be, but the real story has been locked up tighter than the case.

Those Spaniards didn't leave much, Guy remarks as if nothing had happened. I hate to think about all the stuff they melted. You know Las Casas described Mixtec jewelry as 'like something in dreams although made by the hands of men.'

The frog has been priced at three thousand dollars. The workmanship is meticulous. And yet, Muhlbach thinks, I don't care for it. Strange. Gold—the symbol of opulence—to me it's always looked rather cheap. Other metals are more exciting. Bronze. Copper. Silver. And I've always liked diamonds less than agate or amethyst. I suppose that's odd. As a matter of fact I think ceramics have more character than gold. Well, I'm getting as parochial as a basket collector. God knows where specialization ends. Eventually I may find myself stimulated only by late classic Copanahuasta warriors or Ixtlán houses. Early Tlamimilolpan water jars. Kaminalijuyú monkeys.

In any event I can do without the Mixtec. Speaking as a collector whose collection consists of two items, one of which is a fraud, I must say I'm indifferent to Mixtec gold regardless of how valuable it is. And that certainly is valuable. It doesn't belong here. It should be in Mexico. On the other hand, nobody quarrels about the Venus de Milo living in France. And they say half of Egypt's antiquities are in the British Museum. So why shouldn't an assortment of relatively minor treasures sift across the Mexican border? Particularly if they were considered worthless until a few years ago.

Maureen has opened a book. She begins to read aloud:

'Also did I see things which were brought to the Emperor out of the new Land of Gold—a full golden sun, one yard in width, similarly a full silver moon . . . all sorts of objects for human use which are more beautiful to behold than things spoken of in fairy tales. They were all so precious that they have been appraised at one hundred thousand guilders. And in all the days of my life I have seen nothing which so rejoiced my heart as these objects. For I saw among them wondrous artful things, and I marveled over the subtle genius of men in faroff countries . . .'

She shuts the book.

That is from the diary of Albrecht Dürer, Mr. Muhlbach. So you see we are not alone in our enjoyment of these wonderful creations. Arthur is terribly right to deplore the loss. One can't help visualizing the scene in the Spanish royal mint when works of art as magnificent as our frog were simply hurled into a crucible.

Of course the Spaniards had company, she continues. Italians of that period, as you may know, referred to pre-Columbian artifacts as *ornamenti dei barbari*. Jade and turquoise mosaics were broken up in order that the stones might be cut and polished and remounted according to the dictates of Renaissance fashion. Thank Heaven our frog escaped. By the way, Claude was inspecting it this afternoon. He said that he had seen nothing to compare with it, either in New York or in Mexico City.

All very interesting, Muhlbach thinks, but somehow she's gotten the idea that I might be talked into buying a gold frog. I can't afford it. Besides, if I did have that kind of money I'd spend it on Mayan ceramics. With three thousand dollars what would I buy?

He looks around.

Maureen, always alert, waits expectantly.

When he inquires about Jaina figurines she purses her lips just for an instant.

You have taste, Mr. Muhlbach. Unfortunately, Jaina is quite difficult to obtain. We have a ball player, who may or may not have come from the island itself, but certainly illustrates the period and style. Arthur, would that be in the bedroom?

Guy obligingly gets up to fetch the ball player.

We move things, she explains. Our frog was upstairs for months, but then Arthur said really we must try to sell it. Between us, I hope Claude decides not to buy.

Muhlbach turns away. Between us! How anxious she is to make a sale. Buy a gold frog before Claude does. Buy a flint scepter. Buy anything.

Is Mayan your favorite?

I suppose so, yes. Those people seem to have been refined and temperate, if their ceramics are any indication. I hadn't thought about it, but—yes, I'd said I do prefer Mayan.

She nods. Most pre-Columbian collectors start with Mayan because it resembles traditional European art. Zacatecas or Sultepec, by way of contrast, provides very little frame of reference. Beginning collectors are seldom adventurous. They tend to be conservative.

What about the sophisticated collector?

He will choose reflections of his own temperament.

In other words, as I learn more about this business I should expect to outgrow Mayan?

Oh no, not necessarily. We have knowledgeable clients who continue to prefer it. Others like to explore new and unfamiliar areas. Arthur believes we've lost several customers to the current vogue for African.

What about you?

My preference? I would have to say West Coast. Although I can appreciate the discriminating nature of the Maya.

Discriminating, yes. Exactly. That's the word for those people. Precise. Ceremonial. Dignified. Intelligent.

Characteristics which appeal to you, Mr. Muhlbach?

Just then Guy returns with the ball player and after one glimpse Muhlbach knows he must have it.

Guy places it on a shelf beneath a spotlight.

The ball player is thoroughly padded, on his knees, arms outstretched like a desperate goalie defending a hockey net. The right hand is missing, which affects the balance. Otherwise it seems to be in excellent condition. Although there's no trace of the famous blue paint the ball player unmistakably is Mayan. As to whether or not he was buried on the island—well, Muhlbach thinks, my guess is that he was. I've never seen a piece like this, nothing that even compares to it, but I have a feeling it came from Jaina. Anyway, the site doesn't matter. My God, it's superb.

After a while, without remembering when he picked it up, he puts it back on the shelf.

Now comes the disagreeable part. The price.

He tries to look at the figure objectively. It's at least an inch taller than the Taos priest and in better shape, except for the hand. The features are distinct, almost no erosion. The costume is magnificent. All in all it would have to be judged superior. Definitely superior. More imaginative, more evocative, certainly more valuable. Then too, prices aren't the same in New York as in New Mexico. But that lost hand—

well, anyway, I won't get it for thirty dollars. Fifty or sixty would be a bargain. A fair guess might be eighty or ninety. I don't know, it could be higher. I suppose I should brace myself for a shock.

How much are you asking?

Nine hundred.

Muhlbach blinks, not trusting himself to speak.

Which is quite reasonable, she remarks with the aplomb of an experienced swindler. On Madison Avenue you would pay that for a molded piece. And what we have here, of course, is one of a kind. Now in regard to payment, many customers take as long as a year.

I need a few minutes to get over this, he tells himself. Varda was right. These people are thieves.

And in cases where a substantial sum is involved we are open to suggestion.

Well, I don't know. I'm afraid I don't have any suggestions at the moment.

Take your time, Mr. Muhlbach. You have a good eye. You appreciate quality.

I could almost believe you, he thinks, if I hadn't bought that fake Olmec. A good eye indeed. But I do appreciate this Mayan figure, so maybe I'm learning. That might be what she meant.

He turns to Guy.

This is a presumptuous question, but how did you happen to become a dealer?

Guy explains that he studied art in college and after graduation tried to establish himself as a painter. However, you can eat bananas and rice only so long. The next step was pasting up graphics for one of the big agencies, some TV modeling on the side, finally going into partnership with a couple of friends. But all those years he kept remembering a photograph of a Mexican Indian mural that one of his teachers had pinned to the studio wall. It was from Bonampak, of course. As a result, he started collecting old Mexican pottery and fragments of sculpture, then as the agency became more successful he could afford more expensive pieces. Next it seemed logical to dispose of the unimportant objects by opening a gallery.

And what do museum people think about dealers? There seems to be quite a furor—accusations of historical sites being looted.

Furor is right. But it's a complex question. Naturally the museums would like to get hold of the stuff.

Aren't their motives different?

There's one motive: acquisition. Forget everything else. All Maya burials, for instance, are pretty much alike, so a supervised excavation won't turn up anything new—just another cache of ceramics. Maybe a little jade. If the stuff is in a public collection more people get to see it, that's true. The rest of the museum argument is propaganda. Look, on one trip through Hidalgo I actually watched government road builders grinding up Toltec columns to pave the highway. Now I ask you, where were the museum people? Wouldn't it be better to preserve those columns, even if the general public never got to see them?

The questions, of course, are strictly rhetorical.

Guy suddenly waves both arms. It bugs me! he exclaims. I hear this garbage about dealers being thieves and I want to grab somebody by the shirt and say look, this is a complicated situation. Exporting pre-Columbian was legal until recently, and with some controls it should be legal again. In the meantime we're saving all kinds of stuff that otherwise might be destroyed.

Do you agree or not, Mr. Muhlbach?

I'm undecided. To borrow a phrase, this is a complicated situation.

Look, I'll tell you another horror story. Somebody I know—never mind who—was on a buying trip through Yucatán and came across some chicle hunters using a Mayan mural for target practice. I hate to think about that. I love this stuff.

All right, Muhlbach thinks, here we have the commercial argument. I'd like to know what the scholars say. I should have asked that nice old gentleman.

Let me qualify what I've just said. Let me put it like this, Guy resumes, because I don't want you to get the wrong opinion. If I had a chance at a complete Maya temple—helicoptered out of the jungle— the whole thing—I wouldn't take it.

Are you telling me that national treasures belong in the country of origin?

Right.

Maureen nods emphatically.

What about Mixtec gold?

If I thought the Mexican government wanted that frog I'd give it to them at cost. But they've got more stuff than they can catalogue, much less display. And the way things are, do you know what would happen if I shipped it back to Mexico? Six weeks from now you'd see it in another gallery.

And at a higher price, Mr. Muhlbach.

At that moment the front door buzzes.

Maureen touches the button. A Chinese boy enters with a big white cardboard box.

Stick around for supper, Guy suggests.

We ordered more than enough, she adds. And you truly are welcome. Arthur loves being interrogated.

Thank you. I should be going.

Okay, come in whenever, says Guy, walking to the door with him. We're almost always open.

Yes, do! she calls.

I will.

Vaya con Dios.

Goodnight.

OUTSIDE the door he pauses to adjust his hat and to look around. The snow has stopped, which is good news. Well, what now? Let's see. Supper might not be a bad idea. All right, I haven't been to the Village in several years. I'll just wander toward Sheridan Square, call Mrs. Grunthe to say I should be home by nine or by ten at the latest, browse through whatever shops might be open, keep an eye out for a decent restaurant. That ought to be a logical itinerary.

So he sets off, accompanied by a much too familiar lump in his overcoat pocket. It's jade, at least. Some form of jade, although probably not of very good quality. What should be done with it? Sell it to a lapidary, perhaps, as Maureen suggested. There ought to be plenty of them in the Village—jewelers, bead stringers and so forth. Saw the mask into a thousand pieces and put it to some honest use. The thought is vaguely repugnant, but worth considering. As a matter of fact there are a number of things to be considered. This has been a full day.

Just then, as he is about to cross a street, he stops.

Was it imagination? Or was that a pre-Columbian hunchback in the window?

He turns around.

And there, wearing a shaman's helmet, tormented and unspeakably alone in the midst of an incredible display of bric-a-brac, squats the hunchback—lips parted as though moaning, peering up at the world through tilted coffee bean eyes. Above him, like an insult, an arch of gold letters on the glass spells out the name of this emporium:

CHARLOTTE'S CURIOSITY CORNER

He approaches the entrance just as an enormously fat woman in a sleazy Mother Hubbard is about to pull the shade. She hesitates for a long moment, watching him suspiciously.

He points at the hunchback.

She is still doubtful, but at last opens the door.

After taking off his hat Muhlbach steps inside. And suddenly she looks familiar. Was she at the museum? No. Maybe in a bookstore. Well, it's not important.

I won't stay long. That red clay figure interests me.

She waddles toward the window, sighing with effort.

Ah! That sigh. The auction. Yes. She was dressed in jeans and a sweatshirt and was bidding on everything but dropping out as the price went up.

Now she bends ponderously across the tarnished candlesticks and dusty plates and crystal and peppercorn trinkets. Muhlbach, holding his breath, decides to gaze around the shop rather than observe the motion of those colossal parts. If she goes down everything on earth will follow.

Sighing like a brontosaurus she backs out of the window with the hunchback mashed in a steamy embrace. She blows off the dust.

This here is from Mexico. What they call the Colima civilization, she adds, handing the statue to him.

I know.

Most people, they don't, which is the reason I told you. Seems to me I saw you at the auction last week sitting with Mr. Holmgren.

Yes, I was there. You're acquainted with Holmgren, are you? That's a coincidence.

No. Certain folks turn up certain places sure as the devil. Anyhow, nothing surprises me anymore. I'm Charlotte, in case you wondered. Mister, you remind me of my husband. I don't know why, because you don't look like him. You got relatives in Tulsa by chance?

None that I recall. Is your husband from Tulsa?

Charlotte brushes the dust from her hands. Yup. He was lost at sea during the war. Torpedoed. The Germans sank him.

Unquestionably a torpedoed husband deserves some sort of comment. But everything that comes to mind sounds ludicrous, so after a sympathetic nod he begins to examine the hunchback. The piece feels authentic. Eroded. Blunt. He runs his fingertips around the burnished surface and stares at the manganese dioxide flowers. Or could those be spots of paint?

You a professor?

Why do you ask?

Thought you might be, the way you act.

I'm a collector, in a small way.

I got some others if you want to see them.

Yes, but you were about to close.

That's okay. After you get as old as I am a few minutes don't seem like much.

She waddles past a beaded lamp to a spavined corduroy sofa. On the center cushion, tense with deceit, sits an ugly gray Nopiloa fake.

I paid an arm and a leg for that, she announces. So don't try to diddle me on the price.

She can't be serious, the thing is clearly a fraud. Yet there she stands, wheezing with satisfaction. Well, no question about the Nopiloa. The question is whether she's trying to palm off a piece of junk or whether she herself has been swindled.

I'm afraid it's a copy, he remarks.

Charlotte responds to this accusation by continuing to breathe. Then, with the peculiar majesty bequeathed to those who are uncommonly fat, she answers:

Mister, you sure remind me of my husband—the son of a bitch. Thought he was better than me because he went to college. This here is a real old genuine Mexican idol. So don't you tell me. Understand? I been in business at this locale twenty years next August and you can ask anybody. I never gypped a soul in my life. Maybe I'm overweight and I don't have some classy Park Avenue showroom, but by God I never sold one thing that wasn't what I said it was. Ask anybody.

Muhlbach gets ready to leave.

Charlotte turns around with surprising agility and proceeds deeper into her nest of curiosities, talking as she goes:

I'm going to let you see the others because I said I would. I do like I say—not like some people. I guess you're a pretty smart man, mister, dressed the way you are, but I could tell you a couple of things. One thing you ought to learn is there's more to life than having money for fancy cars and living in a big house with servants and sending your kids to private school. I worked all my life and I'm not ashamed of it. I'll tell you that much.

I've touched the button, Muhlbach thinks. All I can do is keep quiet.

Charlotte plunges forward as lightly as a rhinoceros. Muhlbach follows reluctantly with his hands folded behind his back.

Cartons of mildewed books. Phonograph records. Embroidered pillows. Chinaware. Silver goblets. Musical instruments. Clocks, coal scuttles, clothing. The oldest sewing machine in captivity. A Persian rug. More Persian rugs. A fortune in Persian rugs.

The light grows dim. A rancid odor suggests that they are approaching the toilet.

At last she comes to a halt and bends over, once again presenting that formidable bulwark. Muhlbach studies the ceiling, though there's not much to look at except a labyrinth of pipes. The plumber must have been miserably confused.

From the exotic depths of a steamer trunk Charlotte has brought up a shoebox. Inside this shoebox is a hoard of artifacts—obsidian bird points, axheads, scrapers, jade beads, several unidentifiable objects, a mottled green plaque carved in the Mayan style, and some little soapstone faces similar to Arthur Guy's one dollar masterpiece.

Charlotte doesn't say a word. Her silence is menacing.

Muhlbach begins to sift through this cornucopia, reminded of the knickknacks he used to extract from penny arcade vending machines. The beads and scrapers and possibly the axheads are authentic, although they have no artistic value. The bird points may or may not be old. There seems to be a market for arrowheads, judging from the number Piglett was able to sell, which might mean they are being duplicated. These look too crisp, too fresh. But obsidian is durable. These could be old. In any event they aren't worth much. The plaque, however, at least on first sight, is a work of art. A plump Indian dressed in a loincloth, wearing a necklace and a flowering headdress, is seated on the back of a slave. Another Indian offers him a basket of fruit or corn. Scrolls issue from the mouths of these two principal characters to indicate that they are talking, and they are surrounded by glyphs. The stone itself is attractive, variegated brown and green, with traces of ochre paint or dye in the recessed areas.

Charlotte announces that the plaque is Aztec. Five hundred years old.

The plaque is in the Mayan classic style and therefore is a thousand years old, if not older—if it's genuine. But that's not likely. A plaque as important as this—oh, I'm afraid that would be most unlikely, Mr. Muhlbach. Most unlikely, I'm afraid. All right, he thinks, returning the five hundred year old Aztec plaque to the shoebox, but I must say it's well done.

The miniature soapstone faces are false, stylistically incomprehensible. A touch of Guerrero, a dash of Teotihuacán. A sharp Mayan nose above the ever popular Olmec snarl. God knows what else has been tossed into the pot. A turban which looks remotely Arabic combined with a threatening expression suggestive of Rudolph Valentino. A conical hat apparently modeled after a seashell. An Apache headband. Well, kitsch is kitsch wherever you find it.

Only one of the faces was carved with any knowledge—a Zapotec bat-god with inlaid shell fragments. It might be more persuasive without the tar and dirt packed into the nostrils, but on the basis of style it's not a bad imitation.

Muhlbach straightens up, dusting his hands.

Thank you. These certainly are interesting.

Without a word of acknowledgment Charlotte puts the shoebox back in the trunk. Then she repeats that she has been on this corner for twenty years. He can ask anybody. She has a reputation. These are genuine pre-Columbian carvings.

Perhaps she's honest, he says to himself, but she knows even less than I do.

May I see the hunchback again?

No response. However, she might not have heard. He tries once more.

Charlotte, lowering the lid of the trunk, will not reply.

Muhlbach makes his way through the debris toward the front door. The place smells like a chicken coop.

Sorry to have troubled you. Goodnight.

No sooner has he stepped outside than the door is locked and bolted. The shade comes rattling down.

The night air feels as cold as a gun barrel. After several resuscitating breaths he looks at his watch. Time to call Mrs. Grunthe. Donna should be ready for bed and Otto should be attacking his homework. Mrs. Grunthe is a bit lax about the homework and Otto has been probing this weakness.

Otto gets to the telephone first and it is apparent that somehow he has done her in again. A background of neighing horses, shots, screams and the retreating thunder of hooves tells an all too familiar story.

Why aren't you doing your homework?

Otto sounds plaintive. I am.

And just what is that opera I hear?

What opera?

Never mind. Let me speak to Mrs. Grunthe.

She's gone to the bathroom.

Is Donna in bed?

I guess so.

All right. Now listen to me. I want you to turn off that television set. Not five minutes from now, but right now. Get busy on those books.

There is a long silence. Otto tries frantically to think of some reason to avoid the assignment.

Do you hear me?

Yeah.

Then what do you say?

Okay.

I want you to get started on that homework. No fooling.

Okay, okay.

I expect to be home by nine or ten. Is everything all right?

Sure. Did you think the house had caught fire? Holy smoke! Otto chortles over this brilliant response.

Have there been any phone calls?

Just you.

If the doorbell rings I don't want you answering it. Call Mrs. Grunthe.

You've told me that about a billion times.

Is Donna asleep?

You already asked me. How should I know?

All right. When Mrs. Grunthe gets out of the bathroom tell her I'll eat before coming home.

Can do.

I wanted to call and check up.

No problem.

Muhlbach listens a moment. A series of explosions followed by somebody shouting 'Corporal! General Crook wants to see you at once!'

Otto? As soon as we finish talking I want you to turn that thing off. Do you hear me?

I got you, I got you. Good grief!

The message has been received, but how long before Otto opens his books is another matter. Crook will be fighting all the way. I could call again in a few minutes, Muhlbach thinks, but that wouldn't accomplish much because he'd turn down the volume. Well, at least we understand each other.

Goodnight, son.

Okay, goodnight.

And now? It must be time to eat. But what do I want? he asks himself. A dish hot enough to melt the snow. Bouillabaisse? Scaloppine? No, something spicy. Well, the answer is obvious. A Mexican plate.

He consults the telephone book. Mexican restaurants are always El this or La that. And La Mariposa is only a few blocks, probably near Macdougal. So it's settled.

But instead of leaving the booth he hesitates.

This is a mistake, he says aloud an instant before Guy picks up the telephone. I shouldn't be doing this.

One hundred a month? Sure.

I'll mail you the first check next week.

Great. We'll put the piece aside.

I've gone mad, he thinks. Nine hundred dollars. What would Mrs. Grunthe say? Not that it matters. Extortion. Unbelievable. That piece should be no more than sixty—twice what I paid in Taos. Seventy at the most. Varda is absolutely right. Thirty, ninety, nine hundred. This has got to stop, I'll ruin myself.

He continues to argue the matter, frowning in disbelief, all the way across Sheridan Square.

La Mariposa, a converted basement, does not look especially appetizing. La Cucaracha, the roach, might be more appropriate. However, it seems to be doing a good business. So good, in fact, that there's a waiting list.

After leaving his name with the hostess he checks his hat and coat. Then he takes a stool at the bar and orders a margarita.

God help me, he thinks, holding his head in his hands for a moment. Almost a thousand. I must be insane.

La Mariposa has been decorated as extravagantly as a Mexican butterfly. Gaudy twisted paper streamers. Dripping multi-colored candles. Flamboyant posters. Cheap tin icons. Paintings on velvet. The mounted and somewhat moth-eaten head of a bull with a pair of green banderillas crossed beneath it like a blessing. Framed photographs of matadors. A sombrero tacked to the wall. Piñatas. Piñatas everywhere. And six manufactured pre-Columbian citizens crouching on a shelf behind the cash register— confidently lifeless, freckled with gold out of respect for public taste, indistinguishable from one another despite the fact that they represent six unrelated civilizations.

Halfway through the margarita he regards these caricatures with somber disapproval: Aztec, Jalisco, Nayarit, Mixtec, Maya, Toltec.

Perhaps La Mariposa would like to purchase an Olmec jade mask which would be a national treasure if it were authentic.

Alvin the bartender is watchful. He looks from Muhlbach to the idols on the shelf.

Alvin?

Yes, sir?

That wouldn't be a Spanish name.

No, sir. Alvino, yes. Alvin, no. But my mother, she thought it was more beautiful, you know. My sister, she's named Louise.

Where are you from?

Mazatlán. I've been here a long time, though. Six years. Will you like another drink?

That's a good idea. Not so much salt on the rim.

Okay, sir.

Alvin comes back with a fresh margarita, but instead of waiting on other customers he pretends to dry the bar. Clearly he would like to say something.

What's on your mind?

Oh, nothing, sir. I see you looking at the statues. You like them?

No.

Alvin promptly shakes his head in agreement. Those are not real ones. They are copies, you know. The real ones cost a fortune.

So I've heard.

Besides, there are no real ones left. They are all fake.

You're joking.

I swear to you, sir. It's true. They are all fake, except maybe one or two. A friend of mine—he makes them and buries them behind his house in a little garden for a whole year. Sometimes longer. Then he digs them up and sells them to the tourists for a lot of money. Oh, if I tell you how much money he makes doing that you will say I am lying.

Alvin, I would believe you implicitly.

Thank you, sir. Anyway, he has the real ones, too, you know? Maybe a thousand years old. Maybe they are older. It's hard to say, because those people—they didn't write books, you know?

And you've seen them, have you?

Oh, yes. If I visit him.

Can you tell them apart?

The old ones, you mean, from the new ones?

Yes.

Alvin nods wisely. It's not easy, but I can tell.

Amazing.

Thank you, sir. Yes, I can tell. My friend who is my friend a long time, since we were little kids, he explain to me how you know. And if you like a real one maybe I am able to get it for you.

I see. Tell me, Alvin, would you by chance be acquainted with Ignacio Cedral?

No, sir. I am sorry. Does he live in Mazatlán?

He lives in Chilpancingo. I'm not sure I'm pronouncing it right.

Oh! Chilpancingo. Yes, I have never been there, but I know a girl from there. Maybe she knows him. Pretty soon, in about an hour, I will be off work and we can go talk to her.

That won't be necessary.

Will you like me to call her up?

No. Thank you.

Alvin is disappointed. A new customer has been beckoning for attention so he goes away. In a few minutes he returns. He pretends that some glasses need to be dried. Conversation is difficult because of a lugubrious Latin ballad on the jukebox.

You speak Spanish, sir?

Muhlbach shrugs. A few words.

This song, it's very sad. General Felipe Angeles. He is in the carcel—the jail. He plays the guitar and sings La Golondrina because they will shoot him.

I see. Then it's about the revolution?

Yes. My grandfather and my uncle, both were in the revolution. Many people were killed. The soldiers have put the people against the wall to shoot them. You like another drink?

Not now. I'm waiting for a table.

You are going to have dinner?

With luck, yes.

You are alone?

Yes.

Oh, that's too bad. It's very lonely to eat alone.

I agree.

Alvin polishes a glass more and more thoroughly.

Will you like to have dinner with a young girl? Because she's very beautiful. In fact, she is the sister of the famous movie star Conchita Alvirez. You know Conchita Alvirez?

I'm afraid not.

She's in a lot of movies. Anyway, her sister is a good friend of somebody I know.

Just by coincidence is she here tonight?

Yes, sir. It's pretty lucky. And I will go talk to her, if you like to eat dinner together.

I'll think about it.

Okay.

What else? Muhlbach wonders. A real pre-Columbian. The little sister of a movie star. What next, Alvin? Diamonds? Opium? Pancho Villa's rifle?

I've changed my mind about that margarita. Let me have one more.

Yes, sir. Coming up.

Alvin doesn't shove. He holds out a gem for your inspection and if you don't want it—well, who's the loser?

My friend, Muhlbach remarks halfway through the third drink, I would like to tell you that these are delicious.

What's more, he continues to himself, I would like to tell you that pretty soon I may invite the little sister of Conchita Alvirez to share my guacamole.

Permit me to introduce myself, señorita. I am a wealthy collector of pre-Columbian art and the sky's my limit.

The hostess arrives. She has a table.

He gets up, leaving a dollar on the bar. Goodnight, Alvin.

Goodnight, sir. Thank you.

He follows the hostess and presently finds himself seated in a corner, quite an agreeable whitewashed plaster corner from which to observe the subterranean world of La Mariposa. Somehow the air is thick with intrigue. Sudden glances, murmuring. Who is that sinister old man with the pockmarked nose? The dignified woman hiding behind dark glasses and frosty lipstick, what's on her mind? Those two whispering giggling girls, what are they up to? How many stories are beginning? How will they end? Nobody can say, unless it might be Alvin who thoughtfully dries a glass while listening to his new customer.

Muhlbach unfolds the menu. Mexican menus never change. Neither do American menus. Well, there's not much point in reading it. A combination plate. Taco, enchilada, chile relleno, rice and beans. Plenty of hot sauce. Yes indeed, that's the prescription for a winter night.

And I believe I might sample another margarita, he says to the waitress.

As she walks away he begins drumming on the table with his fingertips. Those round stolid features, unsmiling lips, Indian cheekbones—where have I seen that woman? Then he realizes that he has seen her only in a book. She could have been the model for one of those archaic basalt heads excavated at La Venta.

When she returns with the plate he asks if by any chance she might be from the Gulf Coast region.

Yes.

Where?

Papantla.

I'm drunk, he thinks. I am obsessed by pre-Columbian thoughts and as drunk as I've been since I don't remember when. Right now I would very much like to be in Papantla. All right, why don't I go? Lots of people do.

He starts to butter a tortilla and tries to think of a reason he should not go to Papantla. There's no reason. He folds the tortilla and takes a bite. It is hot and buttery and tastes of corn meal and he decides that he will discuss the idea with a travel agent. Papantla. Why not? Even the name is enough to bring forth visions of undiscovered Olmec temples. The jungle around Papantla could hold a clue to Olmec origins. Or what about the town itself? The plaza, for instance. Has anybody ever thought of digging up the plaza? God knows what might be under those cobblestones.

He sees himself dressed for the tropics in white shorts and a pith helmet directing the excavation of Papantla. Another Schliemann. Self-taught. All right, just imagine trenches crisscrossing the plaza. The sun beats down. Mosquitoes. Scorpions. Suddenly a shout! The famous jaguar symbol has been exposed. Then a mosaic floor comes to light. Next a cache of jade figurines in a ritual semicircle. Yes. Wouldn't that be something?

But fantasies aside, I really could take a vacation and go there. I suppose it's a terrible place. Mosquitoes, scorpions, humidity—that's probably not my imagination. I won't go. It's a ridiculous idea.

He reaches for the margarita. But before draining it he stares into that shallow watery pool brimming with the opaque magic and mysteries of ancient Mexico. The sun beats down. Laborers hard at work beneath a cloudless sky. Emerald green vegetation. The screech of parrots. Barking dogs. Children. Burros. Flies. Day after day the trench deepens, then all at once a shout—Señor! Señor!

He frowns. Why should there be a shout? It's like

people in movies running around with kettles of boiling water when a woman has a baby. Well, anyway, a shout goes up because a laborer's pick has broken through the roof of a tomb. Yes, that's good. What next? Maybe a flight of steps littered with gold offerings. The steps lead down and down and down through dusty stagnant silence to an unusual throne. Or maybe to a sarcophagus containing a mummy wearing a gold crown unlike anything previously found in the New World—lapis lazuli cabochons incised with symbols pertaining to Atlantis. No. No, that's a bit much. But the Phoenicians had trading posts in Africa and from there the current would carry a boat to Mexico, so why not a baked clay Phoenician tablet in some Olmec tomb? Or suppose we find a Mayan breastplate! That ought to astound the panjandrums—Bushnell, Ekholm, Dockstader, Coe, the whole bunch. Yes indeed, that should set them on their heels. But isn't it conceivable? The Mayans were at war with the Olmecs, we know that for certain, so someplace in the jungle there might be an undiscovered Olmec tomb packed with Mayan tribute. And someplace there should be a clue to their homeland. If Covarrubias was right and they came from Guerrero—if they traveled that far wouldn't it be reasonable to assume they crossed the Balsas? Of course. They must have traded with the villagers. Well, just suppose those emigrant Olmecs brought along a Nayarit musician or a Colima . . .

He stops eating and shakes his head. That hunchback may have been authentic. The Nopiloa, the soapstone miniatures—those were bad. And the 'Aztec' plaque—no matter how well carved—that must have been a fraud. The hunchback, though, just may have been good.

I need another look, he tells himself. I've got to be positive. I convinced myself about the mask and

I can't afford the same mistake. But that wretched Colima dwarf—he's old. I know he is. On the other hand, what makes me so sure? Maybe I'm depending on intuition.

How about the surface? Were those actual dendrites on his hump or did they just resemble dendrites? If I'd had my glass I think I could have told the difference. They looked right and they felt right. I doubt if they were painted. But how long does it take manganese dioxide to develop naturally? Suppose that piece was buried in salted earth, how many years before those spots developed? I don't know enough, that's the trouble.

Say it's a good piece—how much would it be worth? In other words, assuming she doesn't slam the door in my face, how much am I willing to pay for it? How badly do I want it? Why do I want it?

He realizes that he has left La Mariposa and is on his way to Charlotte's. He cannot remember if he finished eating. And was the check paid? Then he recalls that the hostess smiled while he was putting on his coat. All right.

Once again preoccupied he marches through the Village with snow settling on the brim of his hat. He feels unable to answer the nebulous questions that leap out of nowhere and vanish like poodles jumping through a hoop. It isn't comforting to acquire a little knowledge. Ignorance certainly is preferable. But he has acquired a little knowledge, perhaps no deeper than a root trace, which can't be lost.

He comes to the darkened window. Behind the icy glass sits the anguished dwarf, bitterly alive. What answers are embodied in that dusty gaze?

Speak! Speak! he commands the hunchback. Tell me everything I need to know.

THE BIG BESTSELLERS
ARE AVON BOOKS

☐	Humboldt's Gift Saul Bellow	29447	$1.95
☐	The Moon Lamp Mark Smith	32698	$1.75
☐	The Auctioneer Joan Samson	31088	$1.95
☐	Laura: The Life of Laura Ingalls Wilder D. Zochert	32938	$1.75
☐	The Viking Process Norman Hartley	31617	$1.95
☐	The Surface of Earth Reynolds Price	29306	$1.95
☐	The Monkey Wrench Gang Edward Abbey	30114	$1.95
☐	Beyond the Bedroom Wall Larry Woiwode	29454	$1.95
☐	The Eye of the Storm Patrick White	21527	$1.95
☐	Theophilus North Thornton Wilder	19059	$1.75
☐	Jonathan Livingston Seagull Richard Bach	34777	$1.75
☐	The Bellamy Saga John Pearson	30874	$1.95
☐	Working Studs Terkel	34660	$2.50
☐	Something More Catherine Marshall	27631	$1.75
☐	Getting Yours Letty Cottin Pogrebin	27789	$1.75
☐	Confess, Fletch Gregory Mcdonald	30882	$1.75
☐	Shardik Richard Adams	27359	$1.95
☐	Anya Susan Fromberg Schaeffer	25262	$1.95
☐	The Bermuda Triangle Charles Berlitz	25254	$1.95
☐	Watership Down Richard Adams	19810	$2.25

Available at better bookstores everywhere, or order direct from the publisher.

AVON BOOKS, Mail Order Dept., 250 West 55th St., New York, N.Y. 10019

Please send me the books checked above. I enclose $_____(please include 25¢ per copy for postage and handling). Please use check or money order—sorry, no cash or COD's. Allow 4-6 weeks for delivery.

Mr/Mrs/Miss_____

Address_____

City_____State/Zip_____

BB 6-77